An Opportunity Arises For Marie

Marie wondered exactly what sort of person would choose to live in a converted barn in the middle of a wood. Rush Wood sounded very romantic. Was Aunt Angela romantic? Marie thought not. Angela was more a racy past sort of girl. Marie had tried asking her mother about her older sister, but she had been of little help.

'I really can't recall what sort of person she is, dear,' Sally Stanford said. 'Angela ran away to marry her Frenchman while I was still at school, so I know very little about the affair, or Angela come to that. Father wouldn't have her name mentioned after she left. I was busy studying for exams at the time and Angela sort of drifted out of our lives.'

'You're not serious.' Marie listened in

amazement to this piece of family history.

'I'm afraid so. In order to keep the peace Mother never talked about Angela in my father's presence.'

'But she was your sister,' Marie protested. She could not believe what she was hearing.

Sally Stanford was really big on family values and to learn of this lapse was a bit of a shock.

'Things were different in those days,' Sally pointed out, 'and Angela was only my half sister. We had different fathers. Angela was Mother's daughter by her first husband and there was a significant age gap between the two of us.'

'Even so, to cut off all contact with her?' Marie was still having difficulty getting her head round such behaviour. 'Isn't that a little extreme?'

'I suppose so, but Angela always was a bit wild and when my mother married again after the death of her first husband, Angela didn't really get on with her new stepfather. My father was

FOLLOW YOUR HEART

Marie Stanford's life is turned upside down when she is asked to house sit for her mysterious Aunt Angela, who has purchased a converted barn property in the Cotswolds. Nothing is as it seems . . . Who is the mysterious Jed Soames and why is he so interested in Maynard's? And can she trust Pierre Dubois, Aunt Angela's stepson? Until Marie can find the answers to these questions she dare not let herself follow her heart.

MARGARET MOUNSDON

◆

FOLLOW YOUR HEART

Complete and Unabridged

LINFORD
Leicester

First published in Great Britain in 2010

First Linford Edition
published 2010

British Library CIP Data

Mounsdon, Margaret.
    Follow your heart.- -
    (Linford romance library)
    1. Housesitting- -Fiction. 2. Aunts- -Fiction.
    3. Cotswold Hills (England)- -Fiction.
    4. Romantic suspense novels.
    5. Large type books.
    I. Title II. Series
    823.9′2–dc22

    ISBN 978–1–44480–453–9

Published by
F. A. Thorpe (Publishing)
Anstey, Leicestershire

Set by Words & Graphics Ltd.
Anstey, Leicestershire
Printed and bound in Great Britain by
T. J. International Ltd., Padstow, Cornwall

This book is printed on acid-free paper

a very respectable banker and I think Angela liked to shock him by being outrageous. She was always staying out late and going to endless parties. Some nights,' Sally lowered her voice, 'she didn't come home at all. In the end my father washed his hands of her.'

'Was she expecting a baby? Is that why she eloped?' Marie asked intrigued by this aunt who had flown off in the face of convention to marry a much older Frenchman with a past.

'I don't think there were any children. Mother of course kept in touch with Angela and I'm sure she would have mentioned it if there were.'

Until the letter had arrived three weeks earlier, Marie had not even realised her mother had an older half-sister.

'And now Aunt Angela has been widowed and wants to return to this country?'

'So she says.' Sally scanned the contents of the letter over the top of her glasses. 'She's buying a converted barn in The Cotswolds. I'm so pleased she's got in touch again. We'll be able to visit once she moves back to this country.'

'Well, good luck to Angela. I shall look forward to meeting her. I expect she'll be impossibly chic and sophisticated and make us all seem dreadfully frumpish.' Twin dimples curved the corners of Marie's generous mouth, as she looked at the plump figure of her mother busy making more tea and toast.

'Actually,' her mother admitted, 'the two of you are quite alike in some ways.'

'We are?' Marie raised her eyebrows in surprise.

'You're both unconventional, you both do the unexpected.'

'I'd hardly call being an accounts clerk unconventional and I'm certainly not contemplating running off to get married to an attractive Frenchman,' Marie said, adding, 'I don't even have a boyfriend.'

It had been a while since Marie had

been in a relationship. Her last one had ended disastrously and at the age of twenty-four she was still single. Not that her status worried her. She'd seen far too many of her friends make the wrong decision. Besides, at the moment Marie had other things on her mind.

'Angela was always in scrapes at school too, just like you, and she was actually expelled, several times, if the family rumour machine is to be believed.'

'I was never that bad, Mum.'

'You came quite close to it.'

'Thanks for reminding me.' Marie's deep blue eyes were full of amusement at the memory as she picked up a raisin off the table and began to nibble it.

'If your head teacher hadn't been so liberally minded and I hadn't been one of her most reliable supply teachers, I think you would have been asked to leave too — on more than one occasion.'

'I had to do something to liven things up,' Marie attempted to justify her behaviour. 'You've no idea how dull school life can be.'

'It may surprise you to know, Marie, I was once at school myself.'

'Yes, but that was last century.'

Mother and daughter laughed together as they finished the remains of the breakfast toast. Another long day stretched in front of Marie. She looked through the diamond-patterned window to where a bright sun was shining out of a sapphire blue sky. Maybe she would go for a walk along the beach later. She could take Chrissie, their Yorkie, with them. There was always something interesting for both of them to inspect on the seashore and a breath of sea air always made Marie feel better.

'Would you be interested in helping Angela out?' Sally broke the silence that had fallen between them.

'Me?' Marie had turned her attention back to scanning her own post and nearly choked on her tea. 'What can I do to help Angela?'

'She needs a house sitter.'

'Not my thing at all, Mum.'

Sally removed her glasses and hesitated.

'Out with it, Mum,' Marie prompted. 'You know you always take off your glasses when you want to say something important.'

'Much as your father and I love having you here,' Sally began carefully.

'Say no more,' Marie held up a hand. 'I'm in the way.'

'Not at all,' Sally protested. 'We love having you home again, even if things are a bit cramped.'

When Marie had followed the example of her two brothers and moved out of the family home several years ago, her parents had downsized to a more manageable bungalow further along the south coast. It was very cosy and suited the pair of them well, but space was always at a premium when any of their offspring came to stay. When Marie had been made redundant she'd had to give up her rented flat and now her parents' spare room bulged with her personal possessions, which were gradually creeping into the hall.

'I've got several feelers out for jobs, Mum,' Marie said, 'and I'm networking like mad, but it isn't easy. No one seems to want humble accounts clerks any more.'

'I know that, dear, and you have my full support, but maybe this letter from Angela is the very thing you're looking for — a chance to diversify. This barn conversion has come at a good time. Angela is family as well so it couldn't be better. There's no risk involved.'

'I'm not into interior design or anything like that, Mum,' Marie protested. 'You know I'm hopeless with a paintbrush and I can't hang wallpaper to save my life.'

'I wasn't talking about home decoration as a way of diversification.'

'What then?'

'Perhaps Angela could help you find new business contacts or the chance of a job in a different area? I believe she's very well connected.'

'But we live in Sussex, Mum. We've always lived by the sea. I love it here. The Cotswolds is the most land locked area of the country and it's miles away from home.'

'It's not that far down the motorway, dear and we all have to make sacrifices at times. Your father didn't find it easy to get work all those years ago when his firm was taken over. We were forced to move out of London. Sussex was a new experience for us both but we approached the move positively and we haven't looked back.'

'I'll think about it,' Marie promised, but she should have known her mother wouldn't give up so easily.

'Angela says she needs a house sitter while she convalesces.'

'You didn't mention she was ill.'

'She isn't. It's a minor operation, nothing serious. It's something she's been putting off for a while because she's had so much else to do, but she says it will delay things a bit on her side and very wisely she doesn't want her new property standing empty. That's one of the reasons why she wrote to us, to see if we knew of anyone who would be interested in looking after things for her for a few weeks.'

'Where is this barn?' Marie asked reluctantly, 'and how long would this house sit be for?'

'Not long I don't think and the barn sounds delightful, look here's a picture.' Sally beamed at her daughter as she re-adjusted her glasses. 'It's in a tiny hamlet in the heart of Gloucestershire by the River Windrush. If I wasn't on a term's contract myself I'd almost be tempted to come with you.'

'It sounds very remote.'

'I don't think Angela would settle for anywhere too quiet.'

'How do you know?' Marie challenged her mother. 'You haven't seen her for years.'

'She and Claud were very active socially. They were always entertaining and had a large circle of friends.'

'What does she do now?' Marie asked.

'I think she still models occasionally. That's how she met Claud in the first place. He moved in the art world circles and they were often invited to the same parties.'

Marie chewed her lip. Hanging around her parents' bungalow all day waiting for telephone calls that never came was tedious. Perhaps she did need a change of scenery.

'You don't have to make up your mind yet, dear. There's an email address on the letterhead,' Sally said. 'Why don't you contact Angela and sound her out? I'm sure she'd love to hear from you. She went to a lot of trouble to re-establish contact with us and we're all the family she's got now.'

Which explained why Marie was driving through village after village of golden stone buildings, bathed yellow by the afternoon sunlight.

Angela had been delighted to hear from her niece and after several exchanges of emails, dates and details had been fixed up with Angela promising to be in England at the latest by the beginning of September. That gave Marie most of the month of August free to settle in to Maynard's and keep an eye on things.

'I'm having one or two things freighted over,' Angela had informed her during a brief telephone call, 'you'll probably find they're already there when you arrive, but you don't need to bother with any of that.'

The drive up from the Sussex coast had been an easy one and once Marie had left the motorway, her little car had purred along country lanes. She passed riders on horseback and village greens where dogs romped and old gentlemen snoozed in the sunshine. After the hustle and bustle of the past few weeks Marie felt as though she'd driven through some sort of time warp, back to the days when life was lived at a gentler pace.

For the first time in ages she was

tempted to sing as she drove along. There'd been very little to sing about since the company she worked for had been affected by the banking crisis and Marie had been offered redundancy. It was a common enough story these days and Marie had been determined not to let things get her down. All the same it had been a strain pretending to her parents that everything was fine.

She glanced at her dashboard as the car gave a little shudder. The needle on the petrol gauge was hovering danger-ously close to empty. As she drove around the next corner Marie spotted a small garage tucked away behind a spreading elm. She pulled in. The forecourt was a mass of geranium tubs and scarlet flowers spilled out of little barrels, creating a lovely splash of colour. Turning off the engine Marie got out of the driver's seat to stretch her legs.

'Lovely afternoon,' a friendly looking woman in her early thirties, clutching a greasy rag and dressed in a boiler suit appeared from the depths of the workshop. 'Doing an oil change, always get in a mess. Fancy some refreshment?'

'Is this a service station as well as a garage?' Marie asked looking round.

'It's not but you look like you could do with a brew and I'm thirsty. Come far?'

'Quite a way.' It had been a long time since Marie's snatched motorway cup of coffee and she realised she was very thirsty. 'Some tea would be lovely.'

'Help yourself to petrol then while I put the kettle on.'

Marie filled up, then leaning over to the passenger seat, fished out Angela's emailed directions.

'Have it outside on the bench, shall we?' the woman suggested bringing out a tray of tea and biscuits. 'No, Honey, get off.' She nudged a playful Labrador out of the way. 'Don't feed her any crumbs, she's on a diet. What's that you've got there?' the woman nodded at Marie's sheet of paper. 'Isn't that

Maynard's?' she spotted the photo.

'Do you know where it is?' Marie asked.

'So it's you that's doing up the old place is it? There've been all sorts of rumours flying about the village. The latest was that some pop star had bought it. Local folk have been a bit worried about loud parties and such like.'

'My aunt's bought it actually,' Marie explained, adding, 'She's a widowed lady so I don't think loud parties are her scene.'

Marie crossed her fingers under her sheet of instructions. From what her mother had told her, it might be exactly the sort of thing Angela went in for, but Marie didn't want to upset the locals and the smiling look of relief on the woman's face convinced her she'd said the right thing.

'My aunt's not due to arrive until the beginning of September, so I've come to keep an eye on things for her.'

'Well you're not far from Maynard's,

but the road up to Rush Wood is a bit windy and it's easy to miss the turning if you don't know where you're going. The sign is overgrown. I'm always on at the authorities to cut it back but I never seem to get anywhere. I'd cut it back myself only I've been told it would be an infringement of the regulations. Haven't got the right qualifications or some such nonsense.' She gave a bark of laughter. 'Mad or what? If there's one thing I know about it's cutting back overgrown hedges. My garden out the back is a wilderness. Never seem to have enough time to clear it.'

They settled down on the bench.

'Anyway carry on up the main road, well, I know it's not much of a main road,' she smiled, 'but it's all we've got.' The woman gave Marie brief directions on how to get to Maynard's.

'Call in any time you feel like it,' she said, as they finished their tea and Marie paid for her petrol, 'always nice to have a new face about the place, and if you have any problems with the car, I'm your girl.'

'Do you run the garage?' Marie asked in surprise.

'Yes.'

'On your own?'

'Yes, lock, stock and barrel. It used to belong to my father and as a child I was always helping him out during the holidays and at the weekends. I suppose I was the son he never had. Anyway after I left college I tried working in an office but it wasn't for me, so when I inherited the garage I decided to try and make a go of it. It's a struggle, but I've got my regulars. Lots of the local ladies like dealing with a female, it's sort of reassuring to have another woman to talk to. I speak their language. Men can blind you with science when it comes to talking about what goes on underneath the bonnet of a car.'

'You don't want someone to help with your paperwork do you?' Marie asked on impulse.

'Well, I've a stack of accounts need sorting in the office but I never seem to get round to dealing with them. Like I say, paperwork isn't one of my strengths.'

'I'm an accounts clerk,' Marie said trying not to sound too eager.

'Are you indeed?' The woman looked thoughtfully at her for a few moments.

'And I'm currently unemployed. Sorry,' Marie apologised, 'have I put you in an embarrassing position? I shan't mind if you turn me down, only I'm getting a bit desperate for work.'

'I couldn't afford to pay you much,' the woman said.

'That's all right. I could help out on a casual basis while I'm here.' Marie pushed home her advantage. 'Then if we don't work together well, I can always move on.'

'Tell you what,' the woman said after a few moments' thought, 'how about I offer you free servicing for your car and all the petrol you need?'

'It's a deal,' Marie said.

'My name's Ruth Bradbury.'

'Marie Stanford.'

They shook hands. 'Pleased to meet you, Marie. Drop by when you're sorted out at Maynard's. No hurry, any time will do. The bills will wait another week or so,' Ruth grinned at her. 'Now are you sure you know the way to Rush Wood? Here's my card and my number is on it if you should get lost. Remember, look for the woodman's cottage as you leave the village and then take a sharp left. You go past the old saw mill and after that follow your nose. Good luck.'

Marie Finally Arrives
At Maynard's Barn

Maynard's Barn was exactly how Angela had described it. Marie looked at the photograph she had emailed across. A smile curved her lips. It was hardly anyone's idea of a rural barn. From the outside it was modern, light and airy and reconstructed in a state of the art design along symmetrical Scandinavian lines.

It was set back from the road in a clearing that faced south and caught the best of the afternoon sun. At the end of the pebble dashed drive there was a latched double gate and Marie got out to undo it before continuing down the drive, glad the drive was over. She felt stiff after her long journey and was looking forward to settling in.

Ruth had been right about the

obliterated signpost. Despite her clear instructions, Marie had very nearly missed the turn off hidden behind an overgrown hawthorn hedge but once she'd swung down the lane and into Rush Wood, Maynard's wasn't difficult to find.

The garden she noticed was definitely in the planning stage. At some time recently a digger had been used to clear away the worst of the brambles and overgrown shrubbery, some of which was still smouldering in bonfire ash in a far corner of the plot, leaving a welcome patch of land ready to be worked according she presumed to Angela's plans.

Marie parked her car and got out. She stretched and breathed in the smells of early autumn, damp earth, blackberries and briars, bonfires and the tang of leaves about to turn red and gold. A light breeze stirred the woodland causing the starlings to squawk in protest.

For the first time in several weeks she

felt the tingle of excitement creep up her spine and she realised with surprise she was looking forward to her stay. Helping Angela out was infinitely more promising than the dreaded prospect of working in a call centre, the only employers so far who had shown any interest in her job application — apart from Ruth Bradbury. It had been a stroke of luck bumping into her. Marie had known instantly that she and the older woman would get on.

Humming to herself she turned her attention back to practicalities. Right now she had other priorities to attend to.

Her mother had insisted on supplying her with enough rations to feed a small army and Marie knew it would take a while to unload her suitcase and the supplies from the boot.

'You don't want to go hungry, do you?' Sally had insisted as she added yet another home made cake to the more than ample provisions she had already provided.

'Mum, I'm only going to Gloucestershire and I'm sure they have shops there,' Marie had protested.

'All the same, you'll be busy,' her mother had replied, 'and I expect Angela hasn't given a thought to stocking the fridge. These standbys will keep you going for a few days. Now remember to contact me the moment you arrive.'

For someone who had originally suggested she take up this job her mother was displaying an unusual reluctance to let her leave home thought Marie as she'd loaded up her car boot.

'Not having second thoughts?' she teased. 'I could stay on,' Marie offered, 'and keep you and Dad company now the nights are drawing in?'

'After your father's language last night when he tripped over that tea chest of yours, I don't think that's advisable, dear,' her mother had replied. 'His toe was quite badly bruised and you know how men will go on about such things. Now,' Sally stood back with her hands on her hips, 'are you sure you've got everything? Have I given you enough milk and bread?'

'Everything's fine,' Marie assured her, 'I don't think I can fit anything more into the boot.'

Angela had had the keys couriered to Marie a few days ago and as she unlocked the door and pushed it open a smell of polished pine welcomed her. Although Maynard's had been unoccupied for a while there was none of the cold dampness of an empty property about it. August sun slanted across the floor of the main living room filling it with warmth and light. The large picture windows were designed to gain maximum benefit from the sun and if it hadn't been so late in the day, Marie would have flung them open wide to let in some fresh air.

All the rooms were sun drenched and as Marie acquainted herself with the layout of the barn it was obvious no expense had been spared on the refurbishment.

The renovation had been carried out to the highest specification and no attention to detail overlooked. Brightly coloured throws covered most floor surfaces and there were hand-embroidered cushions on all the beds and chairs, depicting unusual works of art.

The furniture was Regency French, elegant and uncluttered. It was a style that worked and Marie ran an appreciative hand over the polished wood surfaces, liking what she saw.

As she walked past the telephone, she noticed the answer phone flashed up a message received. She pressed the button.

'Marie?' A warm voice greeted her. 'Hello, darling. Angela here. I wanted to be the first to welcome you to Maynard's. It's brilliant of you to help me out in this way and such a nuisance that I wasn't there to welcome you in person. Now, you're to treat Maynard's as home. I hope you find everything to your liking. My agent tells me there's a list of numbers by the phone, all the usual boring things like emergency contacts, local people I have accounts with, my legal team and such like. You have my number so call if there's anything you're not happy about. Bye darling. See you in September.'

The message clicked off with what sounded like a kiss. Marie smiled. She'd already decided she liked Angela and whatever her personal history, it was all in the past. Besides which, Angela's offer of a temporary job had given Marie a lifeline. Who knew how things would develop between herself and Ruth? It might only be a small accounting job in a little local garage, but one thing could lead to another.

With a spring in her step Marie walked out to the car and began unpacking her belongings. It took longer than she would have wished and by the time she had finished she was hot and grubby and her shirt was sticking to her back. Deciding on a shower before supper, Marie chose one of the smaller bedrooms in which to deposit her personal things before inspecting the bathrooms.

Spoilt for choice, Marie decided to save the delights of the sunken marble bath for when she had more time to indulge herself in the luxury of a personal jacuzzi surrounded by aromatherapy candles. Instead she opted for the efficiency of the power shower and soon the grime of the day was being washed away in a cloud of pine-scented steam. As with everything else, Angela had not stinted on the linen and the airing cupboard revealed shelves of the fluffiest white towelling and generous supplies of Egyptian cotton bed linen.

Wrapping a guest towel around her hair, Marie snuggled into one of the voluminous bathrobes, before choosing sheets and pillowcases for the bed.

Deciding she could really get used to a life of luxury, Marie blow dried her hair then shrugged on a clean T-shirt and floral skirt. Her stomach was beginning to let her know it had been a long time since she'd shared tea and biscuits with Ruth outside the garage.

Thankful now that her mother had been so generous with her catering supplies Marie headed for the breakfast bar in the open plan kitchen. Sally had been right Marie thought as she inspected the cupboards.

Angela had catered for every physical need but when it had come to matters of the stomach, the fridge was bare and there was nothing on the shelves in the cupboards.

'Probably used to an army of staff,' Marie said out loud as she switched on the radio for the company and set about making herself a quick snack.

Using the time it took for her lasagne to heat up, Marie acquainted herself with such basics as door locks, heating systems and refuse collection schedules. Angela's agent had done a thorough job and Marie was glad she had arranged to work on a causal basis for Ruth, otherwise there wouldn't have been much to occupy her time.

Angela had indicated that the garden was due for a professional makeover, so Marie's help wouldn't be needed there and as far as Marie could ascertain, the decoration of the house was completely finished.

She stumbled across two packing cases and a trunk in a storeroom by the downstairs cloakroom. They bore French delivery labels and Marie presumed they contained some of Angela's personal effects.

She was inspecting the list of local contacts pinned to the notice board on the wall above the telephone, when its shrill ring made her jump.

'You didn't call,' were her mother's first words before Marie had barely lifted up the receiver.

'Sorry, Mum,' Marie apologised realising with a guilty start it had completely slipped her mind. After living on her own for so long, she had forgotten how her mother fussed over things like arrival times and information updates. 'I arrived safely and I'm just heating up some of your delicious lasagne. You were right about Angela. There isn't a scrap of food in the place,' she said, hoping the praise would mollify and distract her mother.

'I told you so.' The strategy worked, as her mother added in a softer voice, 'Now make sure the lasagne is piping hot, won't you, and have a proper dessert. There's some apple tart in one of the boxes and some of that cheese you like and if you're still hungry there's a bar of chocolate too.'

'Will do,' Marie replied. Her waistbands had been getting steadily tighter while she'd been living with her mother and Marie decided a diet of salads and fresh vegetables might be called for once she'd finished her mother's supplies.

'Have you heard from Angela?' Sally asked.

'There was a telephone message to welcome me. It's really lovely here, Mum, you should see it. No expense has been spared. I'll email you some photos when I've sorted out my laptop.'

'I look forward to seeing them.'

'Someone's put in a lot of work on the redecoration.'

'I think Claud was the sort of man who liked to live well,' her mother acknowledged, 'I expect Angela followed his example.'

'What did he do — Claud?' Marie asked.

'He was an art connoisseur, I think. To be honest I'm not sure, anyway it was something in the art world. Now don't forget, give me a call if you want anything. I'd better go, darling, your father's looking hungry. He's grumpy because his toe's playing up,' Sally whispered down the line.

'Bye, Mum. Love to Dad,' Marie grinned to herself as she replaced the receiver.

Her supper was now ready and she took the savoury smelling lasagne through to the main living room on a tray. The nights were beginning to draw in but she was reluctant to close the curtains. The early evening shadows from the distant wood were the comforting sort, not menacing and Marie wondered about the wildlife. Perhaps she'd get up early in the morning to see if there were any deer roaming the grounds.

She smothered a monster yawn with a smile. It had been a long day and any thoughts of rising before sunrise would have to be put on hold she decided. She was a girl who liked her beauty sleep and the prospect of the snowy pillows and cool sheets on her bed was proving too much of a temptation to resist.

Clearing up in the kitchen and making sure all the doors were properly locked Marie headed upstairs. She fell asleep the moment her head touched the pillow.

Marie Is Being Watched

Jed Soames' mobile bleeped as he was checking through his outstanding emails. He glanced at the caller destination. It was Ruth Bradbury.

'Hi there,' her voice boomed down the line, 'not interrupting things am I?'

'Ruth, no,' he leaned back in his chair, a smile on his face, 'what can I do for you?'

He switched his attention from his laptop to Ruth.

'Had your mother's car in for it's annual service today. Just checking, do I send the bill to you as usual?' she asked.

'Please. Was there much wrong with it?'

'Hardly a thing. I tightened up the odd nut and bolt and gave her a new set of tyres as the front ones were a bit worn. That should see her through for another year. She's a very gentle driver and hardly does any mileage. Wish all my customers were as low maintenance.'

'So she's OK for another year?'

'And some.' Ruth's voice softened. 'My problem is inventing reasons for not presenting her with a bill. It gets more difficult every year.'

'Can't you do the old 'behind with my paperwork' thing on her? It seems to have worked in the past,' Jed suggested.

'I'll try,' Ruth said, 'but your mother's as sharp as a new pin. Gossip gets around here in no time at all and she's bound to hear my news.'

'What's the latest?' Jed asked.

'I've appointed a new accounts clerk on a temporary basis.'

'Not before time. If that mountain of unpaid bills gets any higher in your back office, you won't be able to see out of the windows. They're a health hazard as it is.'

'Don't be so cheeky or I'll set your sister on you.'

Jed grinned. Ruth could be guaranteed to brighten up the dullest day.

'Anyway,' she continued, 'this girl's lost her job and is desperate for work. She was very keen, so we've done a deal.'

'Anyone I know?' Jed asked. He enjoyed talking to Ruth. She was an old friend of his sister's and a good contact. Not much went on locally without her knowing about it.

'You might know of her. Her name's Marie Stanford.'

Jed sat up straight.

'Did you say Marie Stanford?'

'Yes.'

He tapped the name into his laptop. Moments later he had downloaded a photo of a girl with wide deep blue eyes, ash blonde hair and a more than passing resemblance to Angela Dubois.

'She was telling me, it's her aunt who's bought Maynard's,' Ruth was saying. 'You know — up in Rush Wood?'

'Yes, I know,' Jed replied, 'but I

thought the work on it wasn't finished.'

'Apparently Marie is house sitting for the rest of the month of August until her aunt is ready to move in.'

'Right.' Jed was busy inspecting his notes and only half listening.

'She stopped by for some petrol and to ask for directions and we began chatting over a cup of tea. I'm not quite sure how it happened, but she seems to have talked me into giving her a job.' Ruth laughed. 'We bonded right away. She's a lovely girl and certainly got a way with words and you know me — always a sucker for a sob story. Jed are you there?' Ruth prompted when there was no reply.

'Right. Yes.' Jed drew his attention away from the disturbingly attractive eyes staring back at him from his screen. 'Well I look forward to meeting her,' he kept his voice elaborately casual. It wouldn't do to let Ruth suspect he had more than a passing interest in Marie Stanford, 'and thanks for doing Mum's car. I'll settle up with you as soon as I get the bill.'

'If things go according to plan with Marie it should be early next week. Cheers.'

Jed sat at his desk, chewing his lip thoughtfully after Ruth had rung off. This news would bring his plans forward by about three weeks. It shouldn't present too much of a problem, all the same, he could have done with a little more time. When Angela Dubois had booked into her clinic for her operation, he had assumed Maynard's would remain empty until she arrived.

He checked out his cover story and nodded. With a few refinements it should still work.

He leaned back in his chair and strolled through his notes. He had only glimpsed Angela Dubois once at a cocktail party. That sort of thing wasn't really his scene but an old girlfriend had dragged him along. What he had seen of Angela he had liked. Besides being elegant, she possessed a good sense of humour. She also appeared knowledgeable on the subject of art.

Jed hadn't known what to make of her older, enigmatic husband, Claud. He said very little and seemed content to let his wife do all the talking. Their marriage had, against all odds, been long and happy. Angela, when she wasn't modelling, had settled well into a life of fine art and exclusive showings at private galleries throughout Europe and America. They were a significant media couple and no event in the art world was complete without their presence.

Jed wondered briefly what the niece would be like. There was very little to go on. His research had revealed that Angela's family had disowned her after her teenage elopement to marry Claud Dubois. By all accounts she had been a bit of a wild child in her youth and the parting of the ways had probably been inevitable.

Jed's grey eyes clouded over as he tried to imagine being cut off from his own family. At times his sister irritated the life out of him and they'd had some spectacular exchanges of views on more than one occasion, but they always made things up and the thought of never seeing her or her children again filled him with dismay. As for losing contact with his mother, his only other close relative, the idea was unthinkable, but all families were different and from what Jed knew of Angela her character was volatile. Perhaps she just wore them out.

Jed turned his attention back to the on screen picture of Marie Stanford. Would she be like her aunt? She had model looks but helping Ruth out with her accounts was hardly the stuff of superstardom. All the same, Jed realised he would have to make his presence in the village seem plausible. There was intelligence in the deep blue, almost violet coloured eyes looking back at him that told him for all her apparent charm and beauty Marie was nobody's fool. He would have to tread carefully.

Jed scrolled down to re-read the rest of his notes. Marie Stanford was aged twenty-four. She was single and the youngest of the three children of Sally and Roy Stanford. Her two older brothers were both married. She was musical and sang in a choir and played the piano. Jed smiled ruefully. No mileage to be made out of that one. He was tone deaf.

According to his records for the last six months Marie had worked for a builders' merchants in the accounts department. Jed frowned. It wasn't much to go on. Marie had, he supposed, left her job at the builders' merchants. That would explain why she was available to house sit for Angela and why she was keen to do Ruth's accounts.

With a sigh, Jed updated his records on Marie's current job status and added a few personal comments. He then opened his file of case notes and began reading up on all he had about Angela and Claud Dubois.

After a quick check through of his list Pierre Dubois slammed down the boot of his car. His packing was done. All he now needed to do was to leave the keys of his flat with the concierge.

'I don't know how long I'll be away,' he used the special smile he reserved for all females, no matter their age. It sat well on his handsome, slightly rugged features, tanned from years of skiing and a life in the open air. 'Family business,' he explained, 'there's a lot to see to.'

'I understand, monsieur,' Madame Rossay replied. 'I will keep an eye on things for you here. I was sorry to hear about your father,' she added. 'Very sudden was it not?'

'Yes.' A shadow passed over Pierre's face. 'He hadn't been in good health for a while but it was a shock.'

'Hastened by the fire no doubt?'

'Hm,' Pierre agreed casually. It wouldn't do to let Madame Rossay know too much of his family history. She tended to gossip and more rumours about his father's affairs, he did not need. The newspapers had been full of the death of one of the art world's most famous connoisseurs after a devastating fire at his country chateau. For a while Pierre had been door stopped until a new piece of news had broken regarding a political scandal and the reporters had finally left him alone.

He didn't blame Angela for checking into a private clinic. He wished he could have done the same but his schedule wouldn't allow it. Life had to go on and he had some pressing bills that needed to be paid.

The insurance company hadn't been too happy about some of the paintings destroyed in the fire and only last week Pierre had been subjected to a most unpleasant interview. It had done no good pointing out that he had not lived with his father for years and at the time of the fire had been out of the country.

'These things can be faked,' the

insurance investigator had said, looking unconvinced by Pierre's explanation.

'Are you suggesting my word is not my bond?' he demanded.

'Not at all,' had been the reply, 'but we need to explore all possibilities and in cases of claims caused by fire, there are always problems.' His smile had not reached his eyes.

'And now you are head of the family?' Madame Rossay persisted, her voice drawing Pierre's attention back to the present.

She was not a woman to be put off by Pierre's reticence about his personal life.

Pierre shook his head. 'There is no family to be head of, Madame.'

'Your mother . . . '

'My parents were divorced,' he said abruptly cutting her off as he opened the driver's door, anxious to be on his way. 'I'll let you know when I expect to be back.'

'As you wish.' Madame Rossay watched him drive off in an expensive roar of his car's engine. She had no doubt that during his absence, her time would be fully occupied explaining to his numerous girlfriends that Monsieur Dubois was away and no, she didn't know when he was expected to return.

Pierre slid a compact disc into the player and let the strains of Mozart's overture to *The Marriage of Figaro* soothe him. It would be a long drive from Courchevel, up through France, then into the Channel Tunnel and on into England. He had one or two calls to make on the way and he was looking forward to seeing his stepmother, Angela, again. He had been the only person to whom she had entrusted the address of her clinic, a piece of information Pierre was more than pleased to keep to himself.

Pierre and Angela didn't always get on, but Pierre was urbane enough to realise it was better to be on good terms with his stepmother, even if he did resent the fact she had married his father and would in time, when the claim had been settled, share the inheritance of what was left of Claud's art collection empire.

Pierre was also a man who enjoyed feminine company and he had to admit it was easy to enjoy Angela's company. In Pierre's experience, English women were quiet and did not dress as well as their European counterparts.

Angela was neither dull nor unfashionable. She quite simply dazzled a room with her presence. He could understand why she had entranced his father. Pierre himself had fallen under her spell. A small smile curved his lips as he drove along.

The family chateau in The Loire Valley would be empty at the moment and there were several personal items he would like removed before Angela could finalise the sale. He patted his briefcase. No one had asked him to hand over his keys. He suspected keys had been the last things on anyone's mind after the fire, and then after his father's deterioration in health, the matter of the spare set of keys in Pierre's possession had been completely overlooked.

Two-and-a-half hours later after driving through the lush landscape of the Loire Valley he was ready for a break. As he approached his father's chateau down the long drive leading up to the turreted building, he looked up at it with sadness. The ancient building scarred the skyline and was a shell of its former self. The fire had raged through the upstairs rooms making them unsafe and most of the ground floor had been badly damaged making the chateau uninhabitable. By the time the emergency services had arrived to put out the fire there had been little they could do to save the crumbling façade.

Parking on the forecourt by the cracked water fountain, Pierre picked up his briefcase and keys. He had chosen his time well. It was the lunch break and no one was about and he had passed nobody as he'd driven through the sleepy hamlet on his way to the Chateau St Georges.

Ducking under the scaffolding he headed around the back of the property. This was his first visit since the fire and to the best of his knowledge it hadn't affected the summerhouse. It was tucked away in a corner of the ornamental garden well away from the main building.

Like Marie Antoinette, one of his ancestors had enjoyed playing at being a milkmaid and her indulgent husband had erected a miniature farmhouse for her, far enough removed from the house for her activities not to disturb him and his male friends during their card schools.

Claud had shown not the slightest interest in the summerhouse and neither he nor Angela ever went inside, which left it free for Pierre to use whenever he stayed with them, and what Pierre wanted now was hidden away in the summerhouse.

He smiled as the keys slid smoothly into the lock. He always made sure the mechanism was well oiled and didn't stick or squeak. Glancing briefly over his shoulder to make sure no one was lurking in the bushes, he pushed open the door and went inside.

Angela Has Her Suspicions

'You are comfortable, Madame?' The nurse asked as she fussed around her patient.

Angela nodded. 'Yes, thank you.'

'Ring me if you require anything.'

'I will.'

The door closed quietly behind the nurse. Angela looked out of the huge picture window fronting on to the lawn and overlooking the bay. Small boats were moored in the harbour, their white sails bobbing in the wind. She loved this part of Brittany. The view out over the ocean from the cliffs was spectacular.

She and Claud had spent many happy holidays here ambling along the beaches or strolling through the shade of the surrounding woods seeing how many wild flowers they could spot.

They would explore tiny tucked away coves, where they were quite happy to have a picnic of local ham, warm bread and cheese and fresh fruit and sit and watch the world go by.

Claud adored oysters and many was the time they had bought them fresh from the day's catch, grilled them and eaten them together in the intimacy of the kitchen of the farm cottage Claud hired every year. He loved Crêpe Suzettes too and used to serve them in a sauce made with lashings of fresh oranges, the recipe of which he kept a closely guarded secret. They were his speciality and Angela used to tease him that he should have been a chef, not an art connoisseur.

For six whole weeks during the late summer they would enjoy each other's company, exploring the spectacular coastline, stopping off wherever their fancy took them.

'No visitors, or telephones allowed,' Claud would decree as they drove from St Georges towards the West Coast.

Of course Claud hadn't been able to totally switch off from his work and several afternoons would be spent roaming through the cobbled streets of the artists' commune. Claud had an eye for vibrant young styles and their enthusiasm excited him. Often too he and Angela would visit the private art galleries dotted along the coast.

He was always hoping to find an undiscovered masterpiece hidden away perhaps in a back street bistro or hanging unnoticed on the wall of a wine bar.

Angela smiled. He never did, but that was part of the fun, the hoping that one day they might stumble across an unrecognised work of art. She didn't know what they would have done with it if they had, but none of that mattered now. Lazy days spent enjoying the charms of Brittany were a thing of the past.

Claud's health had been a cause for concern for several months before the fire. The doctor had advised Angela that too much excitement and overwork was bad for him and that he should watch his diet. Along with many of his countrymen, Claud enjoyed fine wine and his food and he had been horror-stricken when Angela had insisted he cut down on his indulgences.

She turned away from the window. With every passing day the pain caused by the loss of her beloved Claud was easing. He would not have wished to be a burden on her and these days she could look back on their life together with warm memories. What she must not think about was the fire or the insurance claim.

The nurses had told her to avoid stress and wouldn't let her read the newspapers or have a television set in her room, which meant that time hung heavy on her hands.

Every afternoon she took a walk in the grounds of the convalescent home enjoying the late summer sunshine. The doctors insisted she wore dark glasses and a large straw hat to protect her face from the sun. Years of modelling had taught Angela the importance of looking after her skin and she knew it was good advice to stay out of the glare of the midday sun.

She was looking forward to returning to England. There the climate was softer, the sun not so harsh and the rain gentle. She longed to feel damp leaves under her feet and smell the smells of autumn as nature closed down for winter.

She wondered how Marie was getting on at Maynard's. Her niece and her two brothers had not been born when Angela had run away to marry Claud so she was looking forward to meeting them.

She missed Sally too. Despite the age gap the sisters had bonded but Angela's life had been a mess and she didn't want to disrupt Sally's. She would have liked to keep in touch with her sister after she left home, but Claud was always travelling and with her own modelling commitments, it had been easy to let things slip. Quite without realising it, the years had passed. Sally had married and moved away and Angela had lost contact with her.

Now she had re-established that contact Angela was determined not to lose touch again with the only family she had.

'Madame Dubois.' She looked up as someone called her name. A nurse was waving to her from the main house. 'You have a visitor.'

Angela frowned. The one person who knew she was here was Pierre, and he was under instructions to contact her only in the case of an emergency.

'Coming,' she replied with a frisson of alarm.

What had happened now? she thought as she hurried back across the grass. Pierre was waiting for her in her room.

'What is it?' she asked breathlessly, 'what's wrong?'

'Angela.' He air kissed her cheek. 'I

wanted to see you, that's all. How are you?'

'I'm fine.' She turned her head away and adjusted her dark glasses. She didn't want Pierre to see her scars.

'And the operation?' Pierre persisted.

'It went well.'

'Good.' He sat down uninvited and gestured to Angela to take a seat as if he was the host and she was the visitor.

'What are you doing here?' she demanded.

'I've been to see the château,' Pierre began.

'You didn't go inside?' Angela asked quickly.

Pierre raised an eyebrow at her. 'I didn't, no, but is there any reason why I shouldn't?'

'It's dangerous, that's all.'

'I thought for the moment you had something to hide,' he said with a slow smile, 'something you might not want me to see, like a painting?'

'I know nothing about any paintings,' Angela dismissed his

55

insinuation with a wave of her hand, 'Claud kept that side of the business to himself.'

'So I believe.' Pierre did not sound convinced. 'All the same, there have been stories about the timing of the fire being — convenient.'

'These accusations are totally unfounded.' Angela's breathing quickened. 'Claud was scrupulously professional in all his business dealings and for you to suggest anything else is nothing short of scandalous.'

'My dear Angela,' Pierre said, 'I am not suggesting anything at all. There is no need to get so worked up.'

'Then why did you tell the authorities you thought Claud had a private collection hidden away?'

'Because he told me about it, the paintings you purchased on your annual forays to Brittany. How you collected works of art and took them home.'

'To him they were works of art. He liked to think he had an eye for raw talent. He was always buying paintings he liked. They weren't worth very much but he liked to encourage young painters so if he liked their work, he bought it.'

'All very commendable.'

'Is that what you told the authorities? That they were worth something?'

'I only made suggestions.'

'Suggestions that led them to believe the fire had been started deliberately.' Angela could feel her anger rising. It was always the same with Pierre. He knew how to press the right buttons to annoy her, and now Claud was no longer here, Angela was worried. Pierre wouldn't have come to visit her without a reason.

Pierre shrugged. 'We shall have to wait and see the outcome of their investigations won't we?'

Angela looked away from Pierre. He was Claud's son from his first brief marriage to Brigitte. Claud and Brigitte had been divorced after eighteen months and Brigitte's parents, Pierre's grandparents, had brought him up after

Brigitte moved to America with her new husband, where she still lived.

Sometimes Angela wished Pierre had moved to America with his mother. Whenever he visited her and Claud he always wanted something and his visits would leave Claud upset for days afterwards.

'So,' Pierre said, 'you are moving back to England?'

'Yes.' Angela was reluctant to give Pierre full details of her plans, but she had been unable to avoid telling him her new address.

'I shall look forward to visiting you. It's in The Cotswolds, is it not? I have friends in the area.'

'You'll be very welcome,' she replied automatically.

They both knew they were going through the motions, more for Claud's sake than anything else.

'Tell me about your new modelling job,' Pierre said picking up the hand bell at Angela's bedside and ringing it.

'What are you doing?' she demanded.

'I thought perhaps at this time of day it would be nice to take a little refreshment. Some lemon tea, please,' he said to the nurse who opened the door.

She looked across to Angela who nodded.

'It's for a range of cosmetics for the older woman,' Angela began when the door closed behind her. 'There's a big market for that sort of thing these days and I was lucky enough to be chosen to front the campaign.'

'Congratulations. When will you start?'

'The contract is with my agent now. She is finalising the details. Hopefully within the next few weeks.'

'You are lucky to have such a natural complexion,' Pierre said, his eyes searching Angela's face. 'A result of your English upbringing perhaps?'

Angela did not reply. Pierre was listed as her next of kin on her medical records, although technically they were not blood relations. All the same, his presence here was disturbing and expressly against her wishes. She had stipulated no visitors.

The nurse created a welcome diversion by bringing in the tea and Angela busied herself for several moments pouring it out.

'This barn you are renovating,' Pierre said watching her like a hawk, 'where exactly is this village — Rush, was it?'

'In the heart of England.'

'It sounds very rural.'

Angela sipped her tea but said nothing.

'Is the work finished?'

'Almost,' Angela said, 'the workmen are still on site.'

'And the property, it is unoccupied?'

Angela hesitated. 'I have security,' she said, 'but why do you want to know?'

'Because I was going to advise you of the very same thing. It is a regrettable fact of life, but empty properties are a magnet to vandals. You need to take care now you no longer have my father to look after you. He has left you with a great responsibility. I would like to help you.'

So that was it. Angela bit her lip. Claud had been more than generous towards his son during his lifetime. His annual allowances covered all his needs and Claud had paid most of Pierre's bills but no matter how much Claud gave Pierre he always seemed to want more.

Angela's head was beginning to throb from the strain of talking to Pierre.

'I can't talk about it now, Pierre.'

'Of course not. You are tired,' he said as he finished his tea. 'I'll leave you to rest.'

He stood up to leave. 'How much longer do you intend to remain here?' he asked.

'I'm not sure. Why?' Angela looked up at him.

'I am planning a trip to England and I thought perhaps we could travel over together?'

'I may be here until the end of the month possibly. I don't really know yet. I haven't made any definite plans.'

Pierre nodded. 'In that case I'll

contact you when you are fully recovered.'

It was not a cold day but Angela felt shivery after he left. Pierre was of course entitled to a claim on his father's estate, and he would be a wealthy young man. There was nothing Angela could or would want to do to change the situation. All the same, she could not shake off the feeling that Pierre was up to something and the reason for his visit had been more than concern for her health.

She looked around for the eau de cologne she always used to ease the tension headache behind her eyes. Her handbag wasn't where she has left it on the shelf but on her bedside cabinet. She frowned. The catch was closed and it didn't look as though it had been interfered with — all the same, her suspicions were aroused.

Had Pierre used the few moments he had been alone in her room to look for something inside her bag? The only thing of any value in it was the spare set of keys to Maynard's.

They were still in the envelope with the address on the front. It would have been the work of seconds to make an imprint in something soft like a bar of soap.

Marie Encounters A Stranger

Marie's first morning working for Ruth was not going well. 'How long is it since you've done any filing?' she demanded, looking in dismay at the heap of paperwork threatening at any moment to slide off the shelf and on to the floor. She had been at it for over an hour, trying to make sense of Ruth's erratic accounting system, but her efforts appeared to have made no difference to the mountain of invoices at all. 'Doesn't it drive your official accountant wild?'

'Not too sure actually, and yes,' Ruth didn't look in the least concerned, 'fancy a cup of tea?'

Anxious to beat a hasty retreat Ruth hadn't waited for Marie's answer. The garage kettle was permanently plugged in and she was back moments later with two mugs and a bag of cakes. She produced a jam doughnut and waved it under Marie's nose. 'Hot and fresh, bought from Biddy the Baker's this morning, to officially welcome you to Bradbury Motors and to bribe you to be nice to me,' she added, 'pretty please? You're not going to insist on me doing things like filing systems are you?' Her blue eyes reflected her anxious concern.

Marie accepted the peace offering with a reluctant smile and sunk her doughnut into the tea then hastily licked rich red jam off her fingers as it spurted out of the depths of the doughy softness.

Ruth guffawed. 'Should have warned you about that, sorry. Biddy doesn't stint on her fillings.' She shifted some spark plugs and a gasket and settled down on the only spare surface she could find on top of an ancient looking safe. 'It's nice to have some feminine company to natter to. That's the trouble when you work with cars. It's a man's world and there's only so much football a girl can take. Anyway,' she grasped her mug with greasy fingers, 'how're you settling in?'

It had been a week since Marie's arrival and her first chance to visit Ruth. Despite her misgivings, time had not hung heavily on her hands. Various workmen had appeared on Marie's first morning. All needed instructions, which had meant a constant stream of emails to Angela, who wasn't always available for immediate reply.

The local planning department officer needed updates on the state of the renovation and insisted on all forms being completed on an almost daily basis. The telephone was constantly ringing with calls from Angela's friends who were not aware her arrival at Maynard's had been delayed.

There had also been the strange night noises in the garden, but Marie decided not to tell Ruth about those. Not being used to rural life, she decided to put them down to wild animals and their nocturnal activities, all the same, some of them sounded uncomfortably human and close to the house.

'Do rabbits cough?' she asked Ruth.

'Come again?' Ruth paused, dough-nut half way to her mouth, a perplexed look on her face.

Marie shook her head. 'No matter. I thought life in the country would be quiet,' she admitted, 'but far from it.'

'You haven't seen the half of it. August's our quietest month,' Ruth informed her as they munched content-edly for a few moments. 'Been out anywhere yet?'

'I haven't really had time,' Marie admitted.

'Not too lonely in Rush Wood are you? I mean if you need an evening out, let me know. We'll do a film or a club.'

'Club?' Marie repeated in amaze-ment. In her oily boiler suit and woolly bobble hat, Ruth looked like nobody's idea of a clubber.

'I scrub up quite well actually,' Ruth interpreted her look with a smile. 'We'd have to head out a bit of course, but there's a pretty active scene locally. What's the matter?' Ruth picked up on Marie's lack of enthusiasm. 'Don't you like night clubs?'

'Yes, but,' she hesitated, not wanting to hurt Ruth's feelings. 'I wouldn't have thought there would have been much call for that sort of thing round here.'

'Horse racing fraternity,' Ruth said briskly, 'lively lot.' She grinned, 'and you should see my tango. Been watching all the programmes on the telly and they can't hold a patch to me and Racing Billy — he's the local celeb jockey.'

'A boyfriend?' Marie raised an eyebrow.

Ruth turned an interesting shade of pink.

'Not really. No,' she said gruffly and popped the last of her doughnut into her mouth.

Marie finished her tea without further comment. She could recognise a rebuff when she saw it.

'Well, much as I'd like to hear more tales from the turf, I'd best get on,' she eyed up the curled edges of the outstanding paperwork on Ruth's window ledge. 'Goodness knows how long that lot's been languishing on the shelf,' she tried to look sternly at Ruth, 'and you're not going to tell me are you?'

'Slave driver,' Ruth grumbled, ignoring the question as she gathered up their mugs and the empty doughnut bag. 'Don't forget to fill your car with petrol before you leave will you in case I'm not around? Just write down how much you've taken and leave a note on the spiky thing on the counter.'

'Will do,' Marie nodded and making a space for herself settled down at the ancient desk. She picked up the first invoice.

'Hey,' she said in surprise, 'this is only dated last week.'

'Who's it for?' Ruth asked.

'Mrs Lucy Soames?'

Ruth turned back from the doorway. 'That one has to go to her son — Jed.

He settles all her bills. He's one of my best payers. You'll find his address in the book, and if Lucy phones up to ask where her bill is, the official reason we haven't sent it out to her is because we're behind with our paperwork.' Ruth's weather beaten face crinkled into its habitual smile, 'and no one could accuse you of telling a fib on that one could they?'

'Far from it,' Marie agreed with feeling. 'Still here?' She raised an eyebrow at Ruth.

'I'm going.' Ruth closed the door behind her.

Moments later Marie heard her whistling loudly while she attacked something metallic with a spanner.

* * *

By the time Marie emerged from the dim inner office with streaming eyes and the suggestion of a headache she was surprised to realise it was way past lunchtime. Ruth's doughnuts had filled her up and she hadn't noticed the time.

Her footsteps echoed over the oily workshop floor as she looked round.

'Anybody there? Ruth?' she called out.

'Here, I'm underneath the jeep with the dodgy axle,' she called out from the depths of the pit, 'make any sense of things?'

'A bit, but there's stuff there going back months.'

'Tell me about it,' Ruth's voice echoed up from the pit.

'If I've got time I'll pop by tomorrow.'

While Marie filled her car with petrol from one of Ruth's pumps, Honey, her golden Labrador, loped over with a friendly bark and placed a wet nose on her toes as she sniffed at Marie's sandals. The sun was hot and Marie wished she'd worn something cooler than jeans. She had intended doing a supermarket sweep. Her mother's supplies were dwindling and she was beginning to run out of essentials.

Deciding it would only take a few moments to nip back to the barn and change into a skirt and a cotton top, Marie reversed the car back in the direction of Rush Wood and made her way carefully up the lane anxious not to meet anything coming the other way. She didn't fancy backing up to Ruth's garage and so far she hadn't needed to but from the size of some of the farm vehicles she'd seen working the fields she suspected it was always a possibility.

★   ★   ★

The village of Rush slumbered in the early afternoon sunshine. No one was about and Marie made the journey home in record time. Deciding to leave her car in the lane outside, in order not to get blocked in by the contractors she strode up the path towards the front door.

Fumbling for her keys she shrieked as a voice behind her demanded, 'Who are you?'

Her keys fell out of her fingers and

on to the flagstones.

'I could ask you the same question,' she retaliated challenging the man who had emerged from the bushes and was now standing in front of her. She looked nervously over her shoulder. Where was everybody? Normally there was at least one workman ambling about the place. Today there was no one in sight.

'I didn't mean to scare you. S . . . sorry.' He peered at her intently.

'Are you Marie Stanford?' The question was blunt and put Marie on full alert.

'Yes,' she replied before she realised she had made a bad move. If he knew her name, what else did he know about her? 'Are you stalking me?'

'What?' He looked surprised by her question. 'No, of course not. I've been expecting you. But never mind all that. Do you know there's been an attempted break in?' he demanded.

'What?' She narrowed her eyes.

'Someone's tried to force your front door.'

She looked behind her then swiftly back at him.

'What exactly is going on here?' she challenged, growing annoyed.

'I'm trying to tell you.'

'Well you're not making a very good job of it. And what are you doing here?' Determined not to be intimidated by the most amazing eyes she had seen in years she tilted her chin as she looked up at him. Nature could play some dirty tricks at times. What good were long eyelashes to a man for goodness sake?

'My name is Jed Soames.' He waited as if expecting her to say something.

'If that's supposed to mean something to me, it doesn't.'

'Right.' His lips curled slowly in gentle amusement, 'but now we both know each other's names, we can move forward can't we?'

'Not until you answer my question,' Marie insisted.

'Sorry,' he apologised again, with a devastating smile that totally transformed the roughness of his face, 'I can't actually remember what it was,' he confessed.

Marie blinked up at him. She couldn't quite remember what it was either. He didn't look like a house-breaker but it was wise to remember that the cleverest con men could charm the birds out of the trees.

'How do you know my name?' Marie clenched her fists and tried to think straight. Confronting men who leapt out of bushes behind her was a new experience and she wasn't sure she knew how to deal with it. 'What are you doing here? And how do I know it wasn't you?'

'Whoa,' his smile didn't slip. 'That's three questions. I call that cheating, but I know who you are because I've seen your photo. I'm here to introduce myself to you and, er, what wasn't me?' He frowned over the last question.

'The attempted break in.'

'Ah,' he nodded, 'it wasn't. Scout's honour.' He saluted.

Marie refused to return his smile.

'Don't you believe me?' His smile wavered.

'No.'

'Well, that's honest of you,' he conceded, 'and I suppose I can't totally blame you for thinking I was up to no good.'

'I'm glad we're agreed on something.'

She took time out to look him up and down. In his denim jacket and open necked shirt and trousers, he looked like any other casual caller, and in ordinary circumstances Marie might have been attracted to his outdoor looks, but right now she smelt a rat.

'Would you believe me if I said I was as surprised as you to find your property had been interfered with?'

He looked as though he hadn't shaved that morning. Usually designer stubble didn't do anything for Marie but on Jed Soames it seemed to work.

'Are you growing a beard?' she demanded, determined to take him down a peg or two.

'Powercut first thing this morning,'

he explained, 'I didn't get round to shaving. Sorry. I'll do better tomorrow.'

'Tomorrow?'

'You do want me to come back?'

Marie swallowed hard and shook her head.

'Is that a no?'

'Yes. I mean I don't know. Look, has there really been a break in?'

'It would appear so.'

'And it's nothing to do with you?'

'I keep telling you it isn't. Why don't you believe me?'

'You tell me what you think happened and I'll let you know if I believe you.'

'Fair enough,' Jed agreed with his slow smile then pointed to gouges in the woodwork. 'It looks like someone has tried to open the door with a key that won't work in the lock. Was it like this when you left home this morning?' he asked.

'No, I don't think so.' Marie's heart began to beat erratically. She had overslept and hadn't really noticed. Had someone tried to break in last night? Had that been the strange coughing noise she thought she had heard or had it been her imagination playing tricks?

'Can you remember what time you went out this morning?' Jed asked.

'Just before ten o'clock, but it can't have happened afterwards because the contractors were here and they would have noticed any visitors.' She looked round struck by the lack of noise. 'Where are they by the way?'

'They've been called away urgently on another job. There's a note on the door timed at eleven-thirty. I arrived a few moments ago, so that leaves two hours or so unaccounted for.'

Marie inspected the damage. 'Something must have disturbed them.'

'There's quite a bit of dog walking going on round here,' Jed said, 'and there's been a lot of local interest in the renovation.'

'Tell me about it,' Marie agreed. She'd often wondered what the locals did for entertainment before Angela had decided to renovate Maynard's Barn.

'Did you see anything?' she asked.

Jed shook his head. 'I should have done but I didn't. First day on the job too.'

'What?'

'Personal security.'

He produced a card. Marie glanced down at it.

'Are you a private detective?' Her voice reflected her disbelief.

'I suppose you could say I'm part of Madame Dubois' legal team, with special responsibility for security.'

'What does that mean?'

'I look after broken locks,' Jed said with a deprecating smile.

'Then you're not very good at your job are you?'

'Ouch,' Jed winced.

'It all sounds very high powered, and not at all Aunt Angela. Why would she need bodyguards around here? I'm still not sure I believe you. I think my unexpected arrival disturbed you.'

She watched in satisfaction as her words dimmed Jed's smile.

'Nothing to say?' she challenged him.

'If I was a casual housebreaker I wouldn't have known who you are. And I know who you are because I've seen your picture.'

'You have?'

'When Madame Dubois changed her plans I made it my business to update my information base.'

'And you've got a photo of me on record?'

'The insurance company insisted on it as part of their policy. This is a highly valuable property. They needed to know who you were so Madam Dubois provided a photo as reference.'

'I'm not sure that sort of thing doesn't infringe my human rights and Angela never said a word to me about any of this when she asked for an up-to-date picture of the family.'

Jed shrugged. 'Then I apologise, but Madame Dubois wouldn't have got cover without it and that's why I'm here today, to introduce myself to you.'

Marie was still reluctant to take him at face value. 'Angela has left a list of numbers by the telephone and there's absolutely no mention of you or personal security. Now unless you're off her property within the next few minutes I'm calling the police.'

'D . . . don't do that,' he said hurriedly. 'S . . . sorry,' he apologised. 'I always stammer under stress.'

'If you're as innocent as you say you are you wouldn't be feeling stressed.' Marie tossed back her head in triumph.

'Do you argue about everything?' Jed demanded.

'I've got two older brothers, so the answer to your question is yes. And frankly compared to them you are a very poor challenge.'

'That I can believe. Look first things first. I take it you're not going to let me in?'

'Correct.'

'Then if I may offer a word of advice? Get your locks changed.'

'I don't need your advice to change the locks — thank you,' Marie snapped.

'And if you feel like starting again,' Jed said. 'Give me a ring. My number is on the card.'

'I don't think I'll be availing myself of your services,' she said briskly, 'so far you haven't exactly covered yourself with glory. Now if you'll excuse me I've got things to do.' She bent down to retrieve her keys from where they'd fallen on the ground. Her fingers grazed Jed's as he got there before her. 'Give them back,' she tried to grab them out of his hand, then stumbled as she remembered what had been niggling her ever since he had introduced himself. 'Did you say your name was Jed Soames?'

'Yes?'

'Is your mother Lucy Soames and does she drive a little blue hatchback? And do you settle her bills at Bradbury's Garage?'

A slow smile spread across Jed's face. 'She is. She does and I do and if you still don't believe me, why don't you ring Ruth and ask her to vouch for me?'

'Because . . . because . . . ' Marie could not think of an adequate enough reason to dismiss his suggestion.

'And I'd say using Ruth as a reference constitutes a genuine introduction, wouldn't you?'

Marie experienced an absurd urge to push Jed away. She didn't know why, she just knew being close to him felt dangerous — and it had nothing to do with security or the fact they were alone outside Maynard's Barn. She'd always prided herself on being level headed about men. So why did she feel so inadequate when dealing with Jed Soames?

'How about a cup of coffee? Because of that powercut I didn't get my morning injection of caffeine and I'm gasping. I promise I had nothing to do with the break in, and you never know, the miscreant may still be lingering on the premises.'

Marie looked nervously over her

shoulder. If someone was lurking around she didn't want to have to confront him on her own. Before she could protest further Jed slid the keys carefully into what remained of the lock and opened the door.

Marie Learns About
The Arson Attack

'Whoever it was doesn't seem to have done much damage,' Jed inspected the inside of the door. 'You're lucky Madame Dubois had such a sturdy lock fitted.'

'I still don't understand why anyone would want to break in. There's nothing here, only my stuff and a couple of packing cases and a trunk belonging to Angela, and I can't believe there's anything of any value in them.'

'Does anyone else apart from you and Madame Dubois have a set of keys?'

'No, I don't think so.'

'You'd better check with her. Keep it casual, we don't want to worry her.'

Before Marie could reply the telephone began to ring. 'Go on through,' she said to Jed. 'Kitchen's that way and the coffee's in the cupboard over the sink. Hello?' she picked up the receiver.

'Marie? Glad I caught you. Wasn't sure if you'd gone shopping.'

'Ruth? Is something wrong?'

'No, but I've just had a call from Billy,' she paused, 'Racing Billy? Or to give him his proper name William Hammond.'

Hearing Ruth's friendly voice calmed Marie's fears. She relaxed her hold on the receiver. 'You mean your jockey friend who likes to tango?'

'Got it in one. Anyway, Billy's flogging tickets for a charity do next week, are you interested? It should be quite a bash — dinner and dance. I'm going and I thought it might make a nice night out for you too. You know, introduce you to some of the local crowd?'

'Can't find the mugs,' Jed called through from the kitchen.

There was a short silence down the line before Ruth demanded, 'Have you got a man there?'

'Er — yes. Far corner cupboard,' Marie called back.

'You're a quick mover I must say.'

'It's Jed Soames,' Marie replied.

'What's he doing there?'

'He was here when I got back after I left you. Ruth, we think there's been a break in.'

'You're kidding. At Maynard's Barn?'

'Actually,' Marie waved at Jed then pulled the kitchen door to and lowered her voice, 'I'm glad you called. What do you know about Jed Soames?'

'Just about everything there is to know. I've known him forever and a day. Amongst other things he's the most eligible bachelor in town and if I were you I'd get in there quick. He's also kind to his mum, good with animals and children.'

Marie coloured up. 'That is not what I meant at all.'

'You're looking for a man aren't you?'

'No I am not,' Marie objected.

'What do you want to know about

him then that I haven't told you?' Ruth sounded puzzled.

Marie raised her voice. 'I want to know what does he do for a living?'

'He doesn't break into unoccupied properties belonging to aunts if that's what's worrying you. He's freelance, runs a sort of agency, I think, to do with insurance of some sort. Do you know now you come to mention it I'm not absolutely sure? I went to school with his sister, she's a bit older than him and sometimes he tagged along behind us. I mean I know Jed but not intimately. Why do you want to know what he does for a living anyway and if you are interested why don't you try asking him instead of me?'

'I know this is going to sound silly but I thought he was acting a bit strangely. He pounced on me from behind some bushes demanding to know who I was.'

'Well you can trust Jed,' Ruth said firmly, 'although I can't say what he was doing in your bushes.'

'He's not,' Marie began to feel even more silly as she asked Ruth, 'He's not a detective is he?'

'A what?' There was a loud hoot of laughter. 'You've been watching too much telly, my girl. This is Rush you know, not New York City.'

'He's downloaded a photograph of me from somewhere and he knew all about me.'

'Think I told him,' Ruth confessed.

'Told him what?'

'That you'd arrived and were going to do some casual work for me. Sorry.'

'It doesn't matter,' Marie dismissed her apology. Perhaps she was being critical about Jed for no reason.

'Anyway, better go. I'll tell Billy you're on for Wednesday, shall I? Tell you what, why don't you bring Jed along as your guest? Billy won't mind. The more the merrier.'

'Jed and I are not an item,' Marie said beginning to lose patience with Ruth, 'so will you stop trying to fix me up with him?'

'You could do a lot worse than Jed. Bye,' Ruth trilled.

As Marie turned to go into the kitchen she collided with the wall of Jed's chest. She hadn't heard him open the door but he must have been standing behind her for a while. She flushed. Ruth had a carrying voice and Jed had probably overheard everything she'd said.

'Coffee's ready.' His smile gave nothing away. Marie followed him back into the kitchen. 'Everything looks in order,' he began, 'I mean I wouldn't know if anything was missing of course, but there's no evidence of a disturbance.'

Marie looked round and blushed. Jed had washed up her breakfast things and tidied the worktop. Apart from that the kitchen seemed very much as she had left it that morning.

'Thanks,' she nodded to the rinsed crockery on the draining board.

'Don't mention it.' He grinned. 'I had to do something while you were grilling Ruth about me.'

Marie bit her lip. This was way beyond embarrassing. She tossed her head remembering she was not in the wrong here and she was not going to apologise. 'You've got to appreciate my point of view, Jed, I've never seen you before in my life. Maynard's Barn was deserted when I drove in to find you lurking around in the bushes, pretending to have discovered a break in.'

'I didn't pretend to discover a break in,' Jed retaliated with a frown, 'but we've already done all that. What I don't understand is,' he said, 'why the alarm didn't sound.'

'I didn't set it. I forgot the security number,' Marie confessed, 'and there wasn't time to check it. I left in a bit of a hurry this morning because I couldn't get off to sleep last night.' She decided not to tell Jed about the strange noises she thought she had heard. If someone had been prowling around outside it was none of his business and if there hadn't been anyone then she would only look more of a fool by telling him of her suspicions. 'Anyway, I overslept and I didn't want to be late for my first day at Ruth's, so I rushed out and . . . '

'Left a sink full of dirty dishes and an unset alarm.'

'Seriously, Jed, do you really think someone was trying to break in?'

He hesitated before replying. 'Perhaps you'd better change the security code to a number you can easily remember, just to be on the safe side.'

'But why? There's nothing worth stealing. I'm sure Angela's cases only contain clothes and household things. Apart from that, my bits and pieces aren't worth anything.'

'Perhaps they thought there was money on the premises.'

'Well there isn't.'

'A casual observer wouldn't know that.' Jed glanced at the wall clock. 'You'd better get someone to fix the lock this afternoon. Do you need the name of a locksmith? There's one I can recommend in a neighbouring village.'

'I'll sort something out,' Marie brushed his offer aside. She still wasn't entirely convinced his credentials were all they were cracked up to be, despite Ruth's reference.

'As you wish.' Jed had a disturbing way of looking at her with a half smile, as if he could read what she was thinking.

Marie changed the subject. 'Anyway, why does Angela need all this security for a converted barn in the middle of a wood?'

'I suppose she feels nervous after the fire.'

'What fire?' Marie demanded.

It was Jed's turn to look puzzled. 'At the Chateau St Georges. Didn't she tell you about it?'

Marie shook her head. 'I know this is going to sound a bit strange but we weren't really in touch with Angela while Claud was still alive. She only wrote to us after he died.'

Marie saw Jed looking at her arm, and pulled down the sleeve of her blouse. As a child she'd burnt it on a hot plate and occasionally the scar flared up. Talk of a fire was inflaming it now.

'What happened?'

'It happened during the night. They were both asleep. I don't know all the details but Madame Dubois called the emergency services. Her husband had a weak heart and the strain proved too much for him. He died a couple of months later.'

'Poor Angela. Was there much damage to the chateau?' Marie asked.

'To some parts of it, yes. There's a big insurance claim pending for the loss of various works of art. Of course when that sort of thing happens, there are always rumours.'

'About what?'

'Ask Madame Dubois.'

'I'm asking you.'

Jed hesitated then said, 'There was some talk about the fire having been started deliberately.'

'My aunt wouldn't have done anything like that,' Marie's voice rose in anger. 'And you've no right to accuse her of arson.'

'I'm not, I'm only telling you what people are saying.'

'I don't know much about Angela but I do know she was very happily married for years and that she was devastated when Claud died.'

Jed put a hand across the table and grasped Marie's in an effort to calm her down. His flesh was warm against hers making Marie jump as though a spark of electricity had been generated between them. She wanted to snatch her hand away from his, but his hold was firm and comforting.

Jed's voice was gentle as he said, 'I expect that's why Madame Dubois wanted to make a clean break and why she decided to come back home after living abroad for so many years.'

'You seem to know more about my aunt than I do.' Marie blinked at him. The green eyes looking into hers were doing strange things to the rate of her pulse. With an effort of will power she forced herself to think of more serious things than the colour of Jed's eyes.

At the moment she had more questions than answers. Why had Angela written to her mother after such a long time? And where was she? Marie had an email address in France, but that was all. Had Angela gone into hiding? Was someone trying to find her and was that why there had been an attempted break in?

'Do you know why your aunt changed her travel plans at short notice?' Jed asked, slowly removing his hand from hers.

Marie shook her head. 'She said something about a minor operation and that she hoped to be here by the beginning of September.'

'Hm,' Jed looked thoughtful.

'Have you really been employed as a personal bodyguard?'

As little as a week ago Marie would not have believed she would be sitting in the kitchen of a converted barn in The Cotswolds, having a conversation about suspected arson, burnt works of art, suspected break ins and private bodyguards. In the space of days her life had been turned upside down.

'No, but I do have responsibility for security and I'm as much in the dark over this matter as you are.'

'Do you think I should tell Angela about the incident?'

'I'd keep quiet about it for the time being. The less people who know the better.'

'I've already mentioned it to Ruth.'

'I'll have a word with her. We don't want stories getting around. In a place like Rush gossip spreads.' He began scribbling down a number on a scrap of paper. 'Here's the name of that local locksmith I was telling you about. He's one hundred per cent trustworthy. Give him my name and he'll be round within the hour.' Jed stood up. 'Thanks for the coffee. Do you want me to stay until the locksmith arrives?'

'No, of course not. I'll see you out.'

The barn was eerily silent after he

left. Marie watched his silver grey saloon car ease down the lane then breathed a sigh of relief. The ball of scrunched up paper dug into the palm of her hand. Marie unrolled Jed's note and straightened it out. After the briefest of hesitations she began to dial the locksmith's number.

Marie Meets
The Enigmatic Pierre

'You're who?' Marie studied the stylish man smiling at her as he lounged against the door of his bright red Italian car. The number plates she noticed bore French registration.

'Pierre Dubois?' he quirked a sardonic eyebrow at her, 'and I think I must be a sort of cousin. Your mother is Angela's sister?'

'I didn't know Angela had a son.' Marie was still trying to get her head round this latest piece of news regarding Angela's personal life.

Her last communication from Angela had been a hurried email advising Marie to be extra security conscious, which made Marie wonder if Angela suspected something like a break in might happen.

'I am not Angela's son,' Pierre corrected Marie with a frown. 'Claud, her husband was my father and he married twice. Angela was his second wife. My mother, Brigitte, was his first wife. Tiens.' Pierre held his hands out in a Gallic expression of explanation. 'So that makes us cousins by marriage, does it not?'

'I suppose it does,' Marie agreed.

She was growing accustomed to returning home and finding strange men lurking outside Maynard's. Today it was Pierre. He was much better looking than Jed Soames and definitely did a nicer line in cars. Her eyes strayed to the gleaming paintwork. It was like everything else about Pierre Dubois — polished, poised and positive.

There was no grubbing around in the bushes for Pierre. He had been standing in front of her door about to ring the bell when Marie had driven up.

'Angela did not mention me?' he asked.

Marie shook her head.

'When did you last see her?'

'I haven't actually met her — yet,' she admitted. She still found it rather embarrassing to have to explain the relationship and Marie was anxious to emphasise that she expected she would be meeting up with Angela in the near future.

'She is not here?' Pierre asked, assuming a look of surprise.

'No. I'm house sitting until she arrives at the beginning of September. Didn't you know?'

'I have been away. Angela and I have been out of touch for a while. The last I heard she was moving back to England. I had assumed she was already here.' Pierre hesitated. 'There are things I need to discuss with her — family matters, you understand?'

'I've got an email address and her mobile telephone number,' Marie said.

'I have them too.'

'Yes, of course. Look, we can't stand talking on the doorstep, why don't you come in?' Marie suggested. 'Would you like to look round? Angela's done wonders here.'

'Are you sure I won't be in the way?' Pierre produced his wallet. 'I have a picture of Angela,' he said, 'in case you're worried about me. Look, there are my driving licence and credit cards too as proof of my identity. You can see I am who I say I am.'

Marie looked down at the smiling picture of Angela taken on a publicity shoot. She was standing in the middle of a walk-in wardrobe, surrounded by hangers of clothes. She was holding a classic designer gown in her hands and pretending to inspect the seams for shoddy workmanship. It was a fun photo and the same photo she had sent to Marie's mother.

'It's a good picture, is it not?' Pierre asked.

'Fantastic,' Marie agreed with envy.

'When I grow up, I want to look like Angela,' she said with a smile, handing the photo back to Pierre.

'I understand she has won a new

contract from a cosmetic house too,' Pierre said as he replaced the picture in his wallet and put it back in his pocket.

'Has she?' Marie was only half listening as she locked up her car and searched for the new set of keys the locksmith had issued. It was a nuisance having to treble lock the door and she was anxious not to look a fool in front of Pierre. It was necessary to open them in the correct order otherwise the wrong sequence activated the alarm. 'When did you hear about this?'

'Er — quite recently.' Pierre seemed to lose interest in Angela's contract as he relieved Marie of her bags of shopping. 'Let me. You know I feel I should have arrived with some flowers or a present of perfume as a house-warming gift, but I wasn't sure where this Maynard's was, and whether I would be able to get here today.'

'It doesn't matter. I'm glad you made it.'

'I had some business in the area and I've been visiting friends in Oxford. Are you having trouble opening the door?' he asked.

'Sorry,' Marie inspected the keys again before inserting them in the correct lock. 'Still getting used to the new ones.'

'You've had them replaced?' Pierre asked.

'We had a bit of trouble.' Marie deactivated the alarm. 'We think someone tried to force an entry last week.'

'Where shall I put all this?' Pierre indicated the shopping.

'In the kitchen. It's through there. Thank you.' Marie closed the front door behind them and followed him through.

'That is unfortunate — the break in,' Pierre said as he deposited the bags on the table. 'It's such a lovely area. Were you scared?'

'I wasn't here at the time. Jed discovered the damage.'

'Who is this Jed? Your boyfriend?' Pierre asked.

'No.' Marie wished people wouldn't

assume she and Jed were an item — first Ruth and now Pierre. 'He's a business associate. He's employed by Angela as a security guard.'

'Angela needs a guard out here?' The look of astonishment on Pierre's face registered Marie's own feelings on the matter. 'Is she in some sort of trouble?'

'I don't think so.' Marie frowned. Like Pierre she was perplexed and still not sure she totally believed Jed's explanation as to why he had been lurking outside Maynard's. 'I suppose she thought with the property being empty she needed someone to keep an eye on the place.'

'Isn't that why you are here?' Pierre asked.

'Yes, but I'm out at work . . . '

'Ah, you have a job?' Pierre began unloading her shopping and putting coffee and tea away in the cupboards for her.

'Only casual. I work for the local garage, doing accounts, paperwork, that sort of thing.'

'I see. And before that, you lived locally?'

'No. I come from Sussex. It's on the south coast, but I lost my job and when Angela wrote to my mother, asking if she knew of anyone who might like to look after things here, well, it seemed like a good opportunity for me to get out from under my parents' feet. I moved back home when I had to give up my flat.'

'I understand. You are an only child?'

'I have two brothers. They're both married.'

'It seems we have a lot to learn about each other.' Pierre shrugged off his leather jacket. His shirt was tight white and fitted. Marie could see the toned muscles of his arms through the cotton fabric. They were tanned and taut. She blushed and turned away but not before his eyes caught hers. They were deep chocolate brown and full of warmth.

'Would you like to see round?' Marie cleared her throat and repeated her invitation in an effort to recover her composure.

'It won't be too much of a nuisance?'

'Not at all.' Marie smiled. 'Perhaps you should be house sitting here instead of me?'

'Regretfully, that cannot be. I'm never in one place for a long time.'

'What do you do?' Marie asked.

'I deal in artwork.'

'Like Claud?'

Pierre hesitated. 'No,' he said slowly, 'I work in a different area of art. I will tell you about it when we have more time. So,' he changed the subject, 'the guided tour?'

Marie led Pierre through to the living area. 'Ruth, that's my friend in the village, the one who owns the garage, told me that this was originally a barn on the old Maynard's estate. There's a big house further in the woods. It was sold off when the last member of the family died. A consortium owns it now. They let it out for conferences and business schools, that sort of thing. The outbuildings fell into disrepair and the consortium decided to sell them off and that's how Angela acquired the barn. I don't think there's much of the original property left.'

'Very interesting,' Pierre looked round the open plan living room. 'Angela has made clever use of the space.'

'That's what I thought,' Marie agreed. 'It's not very big, but perfect for a woman living on her own. I'm quite cosy here. There's a small cloakroom downstairs and upstairs a master bedroom with an en suite bathroom, two smaller bedrooms and a shower for visitors.'

There was the sound of a car outside. The early afternoon sun caught the silver of the paintwork as it drew to a halt by the gate.

'Who is that?' Pierre asked.

'Jed Soames,' Marie replied.

Jed had taken to calling in most afternoons about this time. They often enjoyed tea on the terrace and Marie was beginning to look forward to his daily visits.

'Ah, yes. The security guard?' Pierre

looked at him intently. 'He doesn't look very,' he hesitated, 'I do not know the right word in English.'

Neither did Marie, but she knew exactly what Pierre meant.

'Cared for?' Pierre suggested.

The contrast between the two men could not have been more obvious. Pierre was very European, his clothes fitted him well and he had the sleek assurance of a man who knew his way around. Jed was wearing jeans that had seen better days. His shirt was clean but by no stretch of the imagination could it have been called tailored. Neither could the standard of his leather jacket compare to the one worn by Pierre. He shrugged it off and left it on the front seat of his car. He caught sight of Marie looking out of the picture window and waved across.

'Er — if you don't mind,' Pierre inspected his hand, 'I think I have spilt something sticky on my fingers, from your shopping perhaps?'

'The cloakroom's that way,' Marie

indicated past the kitchen. 'Careful you don't fall over Angela's cases. They're half in, half out of the storeroom.'

'Dieu,' Pierre swore as Marie heard him crash into something. 'Too late,' he called back, 'I've stubbed my toe. What on earth has Angela got in these cases? They are enormous.'

There was the sound of Pierre speaking in French as he heaved the large trunk out of his way.

'Hi there.' Jed ambled up the drive. 'How're things?'

'Fine,' Marie replied.

'I've brought a spare set of keys from the locksmith. He asked me to drop them by next time I was passing.' His smile of greeting wavered as Pierre emerged from the cloakroom.

'Sorry, I didn't realise you had a visitor.' His eyes narrowed slightly as Pierre draped his spare arm proprietarily around Marie's shoulders. 'Am I interrupting something?' he asked.

'Not at all.' Marie moved away from Pierre forcing him to release his hold.

'Only a small family reunion. Pierre Dubois.' He held out his hand to shake Jed's. 'I am the stepson of Madame Dubois and you I have been informed are her bodyguard.'

'I didn't say that,' Marie stepped in quickly seeing Jed frown at Pierre's choice of words.

'Didn't you?' Pierre registered surprise. 'No matter. I am pleased you are here, Jed, to look after my cousin. I understand there has been a break in? That is most disturbing. I want you to ensure that it doesn't happen again.'

'I can manage on my own, thank you, Pierre and I don't need Jed to look after me.' Marie's crisp retort drew a reluctant smile from Jed.

'You do not want male protection?' Pierre enquired.

Jed's amusement deepened at the choice of Pierre's words.

'I don't think protection is necessary, that's all,' Marie mumbled.

The living room was large, but with Jed's arrival it seemed to have shrunk and he was standing unnecessarily close to her.

'We think someone did try to force the lock last week,' Jed explained, 'but there have been no further incidents so I hope it was a one off.' The expression in his eyes as he looked at Pierre gave nothing away. 'So, is this a scheduled visit?' he asked, 'or were you passing through?'

'I was showing Pierre around,' Marie explained. 'He called in to see Angela.'

'She's not here. I'm surprised you didn't know.' Jed's voice held none of the teasing banter he'd used on Marie.

'I have been visiting my mother. She lives in America,' Pierre explained. 'When I got back I found an email from Angela saying she was moving to England. She gave me the contact address and as I was in the area I thought I would drop in on her as a surprise. It is allowed, isn't it? I know the English like to be introduced, but we are family aren't we even though we have not already met?'

Marie glared at Jed. In her opinion he was being curt to the point of rudeness. 'Of course it's all right and for your information Jed, that's the same story Angela gave to my mother,' she said in an attempt to defuse the tension between the two men.

She tried to signal to Jed with her eyes that any more of this type of thing and she'd be throwing him out — spare keys and all.

'Except your mother knew that Madam Dubois was having an operation. It's strange she didn't mention it to you, Pierre.' If Jed understood Marie's message, he was choosing to ignore it.

'But she did mention the operation to me,' Pierre replied with a smile, 'she also said she didn't want any visitors, so I couldn't check up on her to see if she was still in France or not. Does my explanation satisfy you?'

'Of course it does, Pierre.' Marie smiled at him, 'and you don't owe us any explanations. You're very welcome at Maynard's, any time you want to drop in.'

'Thank you.'

He looked pointedly at Jed who met his eyes stare for stare but said nothing. It was Pierre who looked away first. He glanced at his watch.

'Could I perhaps treat you to dinner this evening as my guest? Both of you, if you're free?' He extended the invitation to Jed.

'Isn't it your bash with Billy and Ruth tonight?' Jed said before Marie could reply.

'Bash?' Pierre frowned.

'My friend Ruth, the one I told you about at the garage?'

'Ah yes.'

'She has some tickets for a charity ball in Cheltenham,' Marie explained. 'It's tonight. It's sold out, otherwise you could have come along.'

'No matter. Another time then?'

'I'd like that, Pierre.'

He kissed her on the cheek and smiled warmly into her eyes. 'I've enjoyed meeting you,' he said softly, 'and I hope we will meet again very soon.' Before Marie could respond he turned to Jed. 'Nice meeting you too, Jed.' He glanced down at the contents of Jed's open briefcase. 'More keys?' He raised his eyes.

'Spares,' Jed snapped shut the lid.

'I hope you do as good a job of looking after my stepmother's affairs, as you do looking after Marie,' he said with a trace of mockery in his voice. 'Au revoir,' he waved over his shoulder, 'I hope to see you again soon, Marie.' He sauntered down the drive towards his car.

'You were unbelievably rude to Pierre,' Marie said, hardly waiting to close the door before she started on Jed.

'I don't trust him.' His mouth was set in a firm line of disapproval.

'That much was obvious.'

'What's he doing here?'

'He's got every right to be here, and he told you, he's come to visit Angela.'

'She's still in France.'

'But Pierre didn't know that.'

'I don't believe him,' Jed said, the expression in his eyes cold and uncompromising.

'Why not? At least he's got a valid reason to be here,' Marie responded, outraged, 'which is more than you have. Or are you trying to suggest Pierre was somehow responsible for the attempted break in?'

'I'm not sure.'

'I really don't have time to listen to all this.' Marie opened the front door again. The smell of powerful exhaust fumes from Pierre's car wafted into the hall. 'Now if you don't mind I have to get ready for tonight.'

'Promise me,' Jed moved forward, 'that you'll take care? I wouldn't want anything to happen to you.'

'Not good for business?' Marie taunted.

'Of course.' A smile curved Jed's lips. 'What other reason would there be for my concern?'

* ★ ★

Marie's heart was thumping painfully in her chest as she closed the door behind him. She hoped he heard her turning the locks. The man possessed an ego as big as Maynard's Barn. So why was it she felt the stupidest pang of disappointment when he admitted his only concern for her was professional?

Annoyed with herself for being so susceptible to a pair of magnetic green eyes, Marie decided tonight was the night to indulge herself in Angela's sunken marble bath. She would light the spa aromatherapy candles she had purchased during that afternoon's shopping spree and forget all about French cousins and security guards who were not all they seemed to be.

She Seems To Have Disappeared

'Darlin', 'tis wonderful to see you.' Billy smiled sweetly at Ruth as they entered the dance.

'Cut the cod Irish accent Billy,' Ruth gave him a playful punch on the shoulder, 'your father was English.'

'My cover's blown.' Billy made a mock face of horror. 'And who is this lovely lady?'

'Billy meet Marie. Marie, may I have the honour of presenting you to William Hammond, known to one and all as Racing Billy?'

With a sweeping bow, Billy kissed Marie's hand. 'I've waited for this moment all my life,' he professed. Everyone around them laughed and several of the women advised Marie to take no notice.

'He says that to all the girls,' a middle-aged lady swathed in scarlet velvet informed her, 'and we all love him for it.' She smiled affectionately at the jaunty little jockey, with the startling sapphire eyes.

'It's my modest charm,' Billy winked at Marie.

'Leave the girl alone, Billy, she's spoken for. He always likes to show off on these occasions,' Ruth's face was also wreathed in smiles. 'I don't know where we'd be without him.'

'A lot worse off,' Billy replied. He looked over Ruth's shoulder. 'So you didn't manage to drag Jed along with you tonight?'

'He said he was working,' Ruth replied.

Marie looked at her and wondered when Jed had told her that.

'Spies don't work in the evening do they? They're not paid overtime.'

'Jed is not a spy,' Ruth hissed, 'careful what you say.' She smiled nervously, 'in case you haven't noticed everyone looking at us.'

'He's working undercover, isn't he?'

'Is he?' Marie asked, not sure she

understood what Billy was talking about.

'We are not talking work tonight,' Ruth insisted.

'All the same,' Billy continued, his irrepressible good humour unabated, ''tis a shame Jed missed seeing Marie in that ivory silk dress, all for the sake of a state secret.'

Marie blushed under the intensity of Billy's gaze. Ruth had put her in touch with an agency that hired out ballgowns for these sorts of occasions and although Marie wasn't in the least vain the moment she tried on the dress, she knew it was the one for her. It clung to her curves, its delicacy lending her skin the texture of porcelain. Her long white gloves hid the scar on her arm and made her feel incredibly glamorous.

'Spare Marie's blushes, Billy,' Ruth chided him as she looked round the ballroom currently teeming with guests. 'I must say you've managed to drum up quite a crowd.'

The reception was heaving with people talking at the top of their voices, anxious to catch up on news and not listening to a word anyone else was saying.

'Is it always like this?' Marie asked Billy.

'Bit quiet tonight,' he admitted with a roguish twinkle in his eyes, 'but I'll get things going later. Now, darling, you've got to promise me the first dance. It's always my honour to open the proceedings with the most beautiful lady in the room. That sure is a dazzling dress.'

'You've already done that bit, Billy,' Ruth reminded him.

Marie couldn't help smiling at the pint sized dark haired Irishman. Ruth had warned her beforehand not to believe a word he said, all the same it was fun to play along with him.

'A dance is a promise,' she said to Billy, 'now hadn't you better go and talk to some of your other guests?' she suggested. 'Preferably those with money?'

'Good idea. Bye Billy.' Ruth grabbed Marie's arm. 'Come on. Let's get some refreshment before this lot drink the place dry.'

'Why did you tell Billy I was spoken for?' Marie demanded as Ruth tried to catch the barman's attention.

'I didn't want you to get hurt that's all.'

'Billy? From the look of him he wouldn't hurt a fly. Were you trying to warn me off?'

'I don't know what you're talking about,' Ruth wouldn't meet her eyes. 'Is this wretched barman deaf or something?'

'You old fraud,' Marie murmured in her ear, 'you can't fool me. You're in love with him, aren't you?'

'Don't say anything to Billy, please,' Ruth implored, 'he likes to play the field.'

'Then he's mad. Don't worry, Ruth, your secret's safe with me, though I may just put in a good word for you while I'm having that dance with him. What say we take these outside?' She looked down at the two orange juices she was clutching.

'Good idea. Follow me.' Ruth led the

way through the crush out on to the verandah.

'Now, tell me all,' she hissed, 'before I get collared by a determined raffle ticket seller.'

'All what?' Marie asked.

'Word is going round the village like wildfire. Biddy is having a field day. She says you've got men all over the place at Maynard's.'

'I don't know what you're talking about,' Marie protested.

Ruth looked unconvinced. 'This is Ruth you're talking to, but if you want to play forgetful,' she added, 'I'm prepared to jog your memory. A sleek red sports car was seen heading in your direction about two o'clock this afternoon. And before you deny it we have a witness. The driver, who I am reliably informed had a very sexy French accent, had to ask directions. He then three-point turned that fancy car of his round the duck pond because like all visitors to the area, he'd overshot the turning, which reminds me I still haven't had a word with the council about that overgrown hedge. Now what gives?'

'I take it you are referring to Pierre?' Marie tried to look as casual as possible.

'Yes I am referring to Pierre, if that's his name,' Ruth replied, 'or have you other Frenchmen in hiding?'

'I haven't got any Frenchmen in hiding, and how on earth did word get round so quickly?'

'Biddy was taking her afternoon stroll with her dog and saw your Pierre drive up. After she gave him directions, she followed him to the wood, in your interests of course,' Ruth explained. 'She thought he might be another housebreaker.'

'No one was supposed to know about that.'

'In a place like Rush, everyone knows everything about everyone else,' Ruth explained briefly. 'Anyway she hung around outside Maynard's because she knew you were out doing a bit of shopping and getting your dress. She saw you come back. Then she saw Jed arrive. Then she saw this Pierre leave. Then she saw Jed leave.'

Despite her annoyance at having her every move catalogued Marie couldn't help breaking into a smile. 'Looks like Biddy's got the whole story covered. Honestly Ruth there's not much more to say.'

'Marie,' Ruth said in a warning tone of voice, 'what is going on? Who is Pierre?'

'Angela's stepson.'

'Ruth raised her newly plucked eyebrows. 'I didn't know she had one.'

'Neither did I until this afternoon. He turned up to see her.'

'And Jed crashed in on the scene?' Ruth's face was alight with mischief. 'Nice one. Did they come to blows?'

'Nearly. Honestly, Ruth,' Marie said, 'Jed was bordering on rude to Pierre for no reason.'

'Have you tried looking in the mirror?' Ruth suggested.

'What on earth do you mean?'

Ruth shook her head. 'Never mind. So why didn't this Pierre person know where Angela was?'

'I don't know,' Marie admitted. 'Actually, I'm not too sure where she is either. She seems to have disappeared. I mean I've got an email address for her, and she replies to my communications, but that's as far as it goes. The last I heard she was having a minor operation in a private clinic then she was taking time out to convalesce. Pierre's got the same story.'

'I must say your family do lead an exciting life,' Ruth said. 'Fires in chateaux, disappearing aunts, barn break-ins and exotic French cousins. What next?'

'Why are you two lovely ladies hiding out here?' Billy was standing in the French windows pretending to glare at them, 'when there are dozens of men inside demanding to dance with you? And who's got an exotic French cousin?'

'Marie has — his name's Pierre Dubois.

Don't you know a Pierre Dubois?'

Billy's smile slipped a fraction. 'It's a common enough name in France I suppose, but does his father by any chance own a chateau in St Georges and does he collect fine works of art?'

'You know him?' Marie asked in surprise.

'He's a bit of a fixture on the racing circuits. Word of advice,' Billy tapped his nose and looked unnaturally serious, 'don't lend him a penny. He's always short of cash. Likes the high life.'

'Don't we all?' Ruth joked. 'If he wants that car of his serviced, Marie, tell him to go elsewhere. I don't want any French cheques bouncing on me. It's difficult enough to keep my accounts straight as it is. You know, Billy,' she squeezed Marie's arm, 'I do not know where I would be without this treasure. She has totally transformed my life. I have a working filing system that even I can understand and I can now boast up to date records which would stand up to the most eagle eyed inspection.'

Billy shuddered. 'Don't,' he pleaded. 'I'm due a visit from the accountants myself next week. You wouldn't like to help out would you, Marie?'

'No she wouldn't,' Ruth insisted. 'Don't even think about it, Marie. You'll regret it for the rest of your life. Marie does not do creative accounting, Billy. Find someone else.'

Billy pretended to look pained. 'I will ignore that remark. Now come on in, the pair of you. There are masses of men in here champing at the bit all wanting to meet the niece of the legendary Angela Dubois.'

★　★　★

The crowds surged towards them as they made their way back into the ballroom.

'Hello there,' Billy greeted yet another old friend. 'Come and meet my darling Ruth and the lovely

Marie Stanford, one of our guests of honour.'

'Now what's he talking about?' Marie demanded.

'Sorry about this,' Ruth made a face, 'think he's built you up a bit.'

'Me? Why should I be the guest of honour?'

'Seems your Aunt Angela was a bit of a gal in the old days and some of this set knew her.'

'Really?' Marie laughed in surprise.

'Yes indeed.' A chisel faced woman butted in on their conversation. 'I did the modelling circuit with Angela about twenty years ago, before she struck lucky and married Claud Dubois. I was younger than her of course, by several years,' she added after a significant pause. 'Must say she did well for herself with Claud. Tell me, dear,' her glacial smile was as cold as her eyes, 'have you seen her since her face lift?'

★　★　★

'What an old crow,' Ruth said as she headed out of the car park. 'Hope she didn't ruin your evening with that remark about face lifts.'

Marie shook her head. She had been stunned by the remark but she was adult enough not to let it blight her or Billy's evening.

'Who was she anyway?'

'Not sure of her name. I've seen her around once or twice. Do you think she really knew Angela?'

'After that remark about face lifts, I don't really care.'

'That's the spirit.' Ruth slapped the steering wheel. 'Bet she was only jealous of your aunt. They say people start to look like their horses after a while. She certainly did.' Ruth sniggered. 'Good evening wasn't it?'

'I had a lovely time,' Marie agreed. 'You must thank Billy properly for me the next time you see him. I didn't really get a chance to say goodbye. He was having his photo taken and I didn't like to interrupt.'

'Will do,' Ruth said cheerfully as she headed out of the car park and in the direction of the main road. It was a warm evening and Ruth wound down the windows. Strains of orchestra music were still audible in the distance.

'That crowd will probably be going well into the small hours,' Ruth stifled a yawn. 'Hope you didn't mind me dragging you away, but I've got an early start in the morning and I don't think my system is up to only two hours of sleep.'

'Mine neither,' Marie agreed with her. 'It's been a long day. Sure you're OK to drive?'

'Fine. I stuck to orange juice. Best thing really when you know you're going to spend most of the next day immersed in the pit underneath the innards of a car.'

'You really love cars don't you?' Marie said.

'I'm a bit like Billy and his horses. I can't imagine life without them,' Ruth replied. 'Trouble is, these days, most of the stuff is so hi-tech I can't deal with it. That leaves me with the basics like tyres and exhaust systems, and a lot of that means getting down and dirty in the pit.'

'Want me to take your dress back tomorrow?' Marie asked, 'I could call into the garage on my way.'

'Thanks. Best drop them in the dry cleaner's first. I mean I don't think I got any engine oil on mine but,' Ruth slowed down to turn into the village, 'you never know. Doesn't the pond look lovely in the moonlight?' A smile hovered on Ruth's lips. 'I feel quite poetical.'

'Sure it's not an overdose of Irish charm?' Marie ducked as Ruth clipped the hedge, narrowly missing the turn into Rush Wood.

'You know one of these days I'll do a smooth left turn,' Ruth grumbled as bits of hedge scraped along the windows. 'Please remind me to phone the council in the morning and give them an ear bashing. Marie?' she turned her head to look at her. 'What is it? What's the matter?' Ruth demanded.

'Can you see flashing blue lights through the trees?'

'What?' Ruth squinted through the windscreen. 'I can,' she shrieked, pressing down on the accelerator, 'and they're coming from Maynard's.'

Another Disturbance
At Maynard's Barn

Marie was out of the car before Ruth had time to turn off the engine. 'Steady on,' she called out after her as Marie raced towards the flashing blue lights.

'What is it?' Marie gasped, shaking off a policeman's arm as he tried to detain her. 'What's happened?' she gulped, desperately fighting to control the rapid racing of her heart.

An emergency vehicle and a patrol car were parked on a patch of land outside Maynard's.

'You can't go in there,' the officer called after her as Marie raced through the double gates.

'Course she can.' Ruth's voice was abrasive and right behind Marie. 'She lives here.'

'Jed?' Marie shrieked spying long

jean clad legs stretched out from the passenger side of a silver grey saloon car parked in the driveway. 'Are you ill?' she demanded.

He looked up at her and blinked as if to clear his vision. 'Hi, Marie.' His grin was a bit lop-sided. 'Is it that late? Had a good evening?'

He pushed back a lock of chestnut brown hair. It was then Marie noticed the angry bruise on his temple. 'Jed?' She boggled, 'you've been injured.'

'Not so as you'd notice,' he tried to make light of it but it didn't work.

'Did you fall over in the dark?'

'Something like that,' he admitted with a wry smile.

'You are Miss Marie Stanford, I take it, Madam?' The police officer had caught up with her and by the light of his torch was inspecting his notebook. 'And you are the niece of Madame Dubois who owns this property?'

'What?' Marie turned on him in confusion. 'Er, sorry. Yes.'

'And the lady in question is not in

residence at the moment?'

'Has there been another break in?' Marie wasn't listening to his questions.

'Another break in, Madam?' the policeman queried.

'Jed.' Ruth created a welcome interruption. 'What on earth is going on? Have we been raided?'

'I'll ask the questions if you don't mind, Madam.' The police officer tried to take charge. 'And you are?' He asked, his pencil poised over his notebook.

Ruth looked at him in exasperation. 'Ruth Bradbury. I run the garage in the village. Come on, Mike, you know me. Stop being so official. Miss Stanford and I have been out for the evening to one of Billy's charity dos and don't try breathalysing me. You also know I don't drink,' Ruth added for good measure. 'Does that answer all your questions?'

The policeman closed his notebook with a sigh. 'Are you sure you don't require medical attention, sir?' He turned his attention back to Jed.

'My head's as hard as a rock. I'll be fine. You can send that thing away.' He pointed to the waiting ambulance. 'Not that I'm not grateful, you understand, but I'm not going to A & E. A good night's sleep will see me through.'

'As you wish, sir. I can't force you to go to. If you can think of anything else to add to your statement, then call in at the police station.'

'Will do, officer and thank you.'

'Keep an eye on him, Ruth,' Mike murmured on his way back to the patrol car. 'He's had a nasty bump. Bit of a run in with a prowler I believe.'

'Did anyone see anything?' Ruth lowered her voice, not wanting Marie to overhear.

'There weren't any witnesses if that's what you mean, so we only have Mr Soames' word for what happened.'

'You don't believe him?'

'I didn't say that,' Mike replied, 'but I'm keeping an open mind on things. To be honest I don't think he's telling us everything that happened here tonight.'

'Thanks anyway, Mike,' Ruth said. 'See you around.'

She watched him drive off then turned her attention back to Marie and Jed.

'Let's get you inside.' Marie was bent forward and trying to help Jed to his feet. He swayed against her.

'I'm all right, really,' he insisted.

'You're as bad as my brothers when they've been hurt playing rugby,' she chided him in exasperation, 'and you're as heavy. Now lean on me. I'm tough. I won't buckle.'

Jed did as he was told and Marie did her best not to stumble against his weight. She could feel the strength of his muscles against the thin material of her dress and his breath was warm on her face.

'That's a lovely dress,' he nuzzled softly into her ear, his words slightly slurred. 'Makes you look beautiful in the moonlight.'

Marie almost lost her footing as she tried to concentrate on putting one foot in front of the other.

'I'll do the other side.' Ruth grabbed Jed's arm and Marie, her head whirling, was relieved when he eased his body away. It was an unnerving experience feeling Jed's flesh so close to hers.

'Did you hear what I said?' he bent his head close to Marie's.

'That bump's unhinged you,' Marie hissed in reply as she steadied herself. 'It's Marie here, remember? We don't like each other.'

'What are you two going on about?' Ruth gasped.

'Nothing,' Marie replied through gritted teeth.

'Then I suggest you save your breath for walking, not talking.'

'Good idea,' Marie agreed. It was important to keep focussed.

Despite Jed's protestations, it was obvious he had been injured. He was no lightweight, but they had to get him into the house in one piece.

Between them they eventually managed to shuffle a groaning Jed into the kitchen.

'Sit down here.' Ruth dragged a chair out from under the table and Jed lowered himself on to it.

'Black coffee is called for I think and got any painkillers?' Ruth recovered her breath first. 'Heavens,' her eyes widened as Marie put the main light on, 'look at the state of us.'

Their hired dresses were covered in dirt and bits of foliage from where they'd staggered up the path, hauling Jed along between them.

'Think you've got half a tree in your hair, Ruth,' Marie pulled a twig out of Ruth's chignon. Strands of hair escaped as Marie tugged and the next moment the elegant creation collapsed entirely.

'That's saved me the bother of taking it down,' Ruth said as she clipped it back into its more manageable ponytail. 'There that's better. Now let's see about that coffee.'

'Hope the dry cleaners know how to get stains out of oyster satin,' Marie said wryly taking in her own dishevelled appearance.

'You're in for a big bill if they don't,' Ruth looked over her shoulder. 'Look out. Catch him,' she cried as Jed fell forward.

'I'm all right. I just need to hold my head for a bit. Feels like a lead weight,' Jed groaned.

'Here,' Ruth thrust a glass of cold water and two tablets at him. 'Take these.'

'You still haven't told us what happened,' Marie put in, annoyed with herself for over reacting to the situation. What was Jed Soames to her? And why should she care what happened to him? He was only a member of Angela's legal team with special responsibility for security — or so he said.

'And we want the truth,' Ruth added. 'Not that trumped up story you gave Mike.'

'I don't know what happened.' Jed's voice was a hoarse rasp as his teeth knocked against the glass of water. 'One minute I was walking along and the next I was flat out on the ground. I came round with a massive headache and my briefcase was missing.'

'What were you doing taking your briefcase for a walk in the woods at midnight anyway?' Marie demanded.

'I still had the spare set of keys for your new locks. I'd been working late and I thought I'd drop them by on my way home. I'd forgotten you were out.'

Marie looked into his green eyes. He looked away first. She knew he was lying.

'Great,' Ruth said as she plonked three mugs of strong coffee down on the table. 'Now there's a mugger out there in possession of the spare keys to Marie's barn. You really are the most awful fool losing them, Jed and you're not spending the night here on your own,' Ruth instructed Marie before she could say anything. 'You're coming back to my place with me in case this person, whoever he is, tries to use the keys to gain access.'

'I can't leave Maynard's. Angela's stuff is all here. That's why she wanted a house sitter. There might be some valuables in her cases.'

'What say we all stay here then?' Ruth suggested. 'From the look of poor old Jed, he's not capable of standing up, let alone driving home. Can you rig a spare bed up for him do you think?'

'He could have mine. We could share the double in the main bedroom. We need to make the bed up, that's all.'

'Right then, drink up.' Ruth nudged her coffee towards Marie. 'Don't know about you,' she stifled a yawn, 'but I'm ready for some sleep.' She looked across at Jed. 'What are we going to do about him?'

'What do you mean?'

'How are we going to get him upstairs?'

'Would you two mind not talking about me as if I wasn't here?' Jed grumbled from the depths of his shirt, still holding his head in his hands. 'I am quite capable of looking after myself.'

'Stubborn as a mule. Exactly like his sister,' Ruth huffed. 'How many bangs on the head does it take to knock some sense into you, Jed Soames?'

Jed raised his head and picking up his mug sipped his coffee carefully.

'I'm not staying the night,' he said slowly.

'Jed, I think Ruth's right,' Marie insisted.

'Course I am, I'm always right,' Ruth agreed with her.

'If someone has got the spare keys to Maynard's, they could walk in at any time. All they've got to do is unlock the door. I'll have to do something about yet another set of locks, but I can't do anything until the morning. I'd feel safer if you and Ruth stayed over.'

'He won't be any good to you,' Ruth said with a sniff, 'if someone does try to get in. But I can be pretty handy with a poker.' She flexed an arm muscle. 'It's all that spanner wielding in the garage.'

'Why on earth did you mention the other break in?' Jed mumbled frowning at Marie.

'I didn't realise it was classified

information,' Marie retaliated.

'And for what it's worth, Jed,' Ruth put in, 'Mike wasn't wholly convinced by your version of events here tonight. You may find him pursuing enquiries.'

'He has no reason to. I was perfectly entitled to be in Rush Wood, even if it was late in the day.'

'You know you really are a rubbish liar,' Ruth said with an indulgent smile. 'You were hopeless at it when you were a boy and you're no better now. No,' she held up a hand, 'don't tell me any more. I don't want to know.'

'But what happened was all my fault,' Jed interrupted.

'You can say that again, but I still don't think you're telling the truth.'

'Shut up, Ruth,' Jed retaliated.

'No I won't. I need to have my say and then I'll shut up. I don't know what you were doing in Rush Wood but I'm certain you weren't here to deliver Marie her second set of keys.'

Marie had been thinking pretty much along the same lines.

'She's right you know. You couldn't have forgotten I was going out. I only told you this afternoon. So,' she demanded, 'what gives?'

Jed still looked woozy as he tried to focus on Marie. 'If you must know I was keeping an eye on the place.'

'Why?' Ruth looked puzzled.

'Is this about Pierre?' Marie could no longer ignore the nibble of suspicion at the back of her mind.

'Look, can we save this discussion for the morning?' Jed asked in a shaky voice. 'I don't think I'm up to further investigation from the pair of you.'

'What you mean is you want more time to think up a convincing story,' Ruth said.

'Who called the police and the ambulance?' Marie asked.

'Biddy.'

'That woman gets everywhere,' Ruth's voice was raised in exasperation. 'What was she doing in Rush Wood?'

'She was walking her dog.'

'She's always walking her dog. She

must have the fittest dog in the county.'

'Did she see what happened?' Marie asked.

'Not sure,' Jed replied. 'I heard her talking to the police, but I couldn't hear what she was saying.'

'Well the whole thing sounds fishy to me,' Ruth said. 'But I dare say it'll wait until the morning. Now are we going to bed or what?'

Without giving anyone a chance to reply, Ruth whipped away their mugs and washed them up in the sink.

'P'rhaps we ought to have a quick look round first?' Jed was still having difficulty with his words.

'What for?'

'I don't know how long I was out. Whoever it was who took the keys may have used them.'

'That's right, frighten the life out of the pair of us,' Ruth complained as she dried up the mugs. 'If the intruder is still on the premises I'm in the right frame of mind to deal with him. Got anything heavy and hard, Marie?' She began looking round for a suitable weapon of defence.

'You mentioned your aunt's things?' Jed had stopped swaying and was beginning to recover his composure.

'They're through here,' Marie headed for the cloakroom and inspected the packing cases.

'Have they been disturbed?'

'No, everything seems fine. I mean, they've been moved, but that was Pierre. He kicked one by accident.'

Ruth hung up the tea towel. 'Not sure if I locked my car, actually. I'll nip outside and check up and park it properly. Won't be a moment. Want me to check on yours as well, Jed?'

He found his keys in the pocket of his leather jacket and handed them over to her, all the while his eyes boring holes in Marie's.

With Ruth's departure the tension in the kitchen tightened. Marie swallowed down the lump of nervousness in her throat. Jed had no right to look so heart stoppingly attractive, covered in dirt and with a huge bruise on his forehead — and what was that he had said about her dress?

'You suspect Pierre of something, don't you?' she said.

'I'm suspicious of him, yes,' Jed mumbled.

'For the same reason I'm suspicious of you?' The words came out sharper than Marie had intended, but she needed to keep her other feelings for Jed well under control.

'You're suspicious of me? Why?'

'You know perfectly well why. You were here when we had the first attempted break in. Pierre wasn't. You tell us someone stole your briefcase but we don't know that. Even the policeman didn't believe your explanation. To be honest, it was so flimsy a child of three would have seen through it.'

Jed looked pale under the harsh strip lighting. His eyes were fixed on her intently and he was breathing heavily.

He stood up slowly. A sharp pain in Marie's back made her realise she had flattened herself against the wall.

'I think in the circumstances,' he said, with as much dignity as he could muster, 'it would be better if I didn't spend the night under the same roof as you.'

'Don't be ridiculous. You can't drive all the way back to Cheltenham.'

'Ruth's painkillers are kicking in and my sister doesn't live far away, I'll stay at her place.'

'No, Jed,' Marie put out a hand. 'Don't go.'

'You'll be all right, Ruth's here and to be honest, I'm glad she is.'

'What do you mean?' Marie's mouth had gone dry. From the way Jed was looking at her, she was having great difficulty not begging him to stay.

He leaned forward and tucked a stray tendril of hair behind one of her ears. His voice was unusually soft as he added, 'You're quite wrong about me not liking you, you know.'

Marie didn't reply. She couldn't.

'Don't forget to set the alarm before

you lock up,' he said, then, turning away from her, walked very slowly, very carefully out of the kitchen and into the night.

Marie's Suspicions About Jed Grow

'Sorry I had to rush off so suddenly. Everything OK?' Ruth sounded her usual ebullient self the next morning, with no trace of tiredness in her voice.

'Fine.' Marie tried not to yawn or look at her reflection in the mirror above the telephone. She had been inspecting Angela's emergency numbers when Ruth had called.

'Has the locksmith been yet?'

'Yes. I've got yet two more new sets of keys and I'm not letting Jed get his hands on either of them.'

'You ought to have a standing order with that man,' Ruth joked. 'Well, only checking up on you. Best get on. If you feel like company drop in, I'll be here all day.'

Ruth had left her ball gown on the bed and gone home in one of Marie's skirts. Marie parcelled up the two hired dresses and took them down to her car. Damp mud stuck to her sandals and she could see where all the disturbance had taken place the night before. There were several sets of footprints and the clear outline of a dog's paw. At least the bit about Biddy being here was true she thought as feeling a bit like a private detective herself she looked around for clues. Although exactly what she thought she would find she wasn't sure.

She could see where the police car had parked, and the imprints the ambulance tyres had left behind, as well as those made by Ruth's car. Jed's too had left tracks. She tried to push thoughts of Jed out of her mind and forced herself to think about Pierre instead. She wondered briefly if he was still in the area.

Had his promise to take her out to dinner only been a polite invitation or would he be in touch again?

Marie frowned. What was it Billy had said about Pierre? Something to do with money, she seemed to remember.

The telephone was ringing again as she went back inside.

'Hello, darling.' It was her mother. 'How are things?'

'Fine.' Marie crossed her fingers. A silly habit but she didn't like fibbing to her mother, but no way was she going to worry her mother by telling her what had been going on at Maynard's barn. Sally Stanford would be down the motorway like a shot if she thought anything was amiss with one of her brood or that anyone was upsetting Marie.

'You sound tired.'

'I was out late last night. Ruth, that's my friend at the garage, invited me to a charity ball. We didn't get to bed until late.'

Marie uncrossed her fingers.

'A ball? That sounds very grand. I'm glad you're making new friends. And your job is going well at the garage?'

'Yes. I'm really getting things straight there.'

'I told you what you needed was a change of scenery.'

'Right yet again, Mum.'

'Have you heard from Angela?'

'I had an email the other day,' Marie cast her mind back to the faintly disturbing communication she had received, reminding her to be extra vigilant regarding security. Angela had given her no other details for her cause for concern.

'Send her my love when you're next in touch.'

'Will do,' Marie promised.

'Well, I won't keep you, I know you're busy. Do try and keep in touch won't you? You know how I worry about you.'

'Sorry, Mum. Will do. Give my love to Dad.'

After she hung up, she strolled through to the main living room. The early autumn sun was doing its best to pretend it was a summer's day and yet again it streamed through the huge picture window. The contractors had departed, promising to return when Angela delivered the final details of exactly what she wanted doing to the plot of land surrounding the barn.

Despite her best intentions Marie's thoughts strayed to Jed. After he'd left so abruptly last night and Ruth had stopped asking questions about his sudden departure, Marie had fallen into a fitful sleep.

Ruth had insisted on sleeping on the sofa. 'No point in making up the double,' she'd said, 'and I wouldn't want you to give up your bed for me. Don't worry. Nothing will keep me awake. Always fall asleep the moment my head touches the pillow. Sleep of the innocent I say.'

Marie for her part had tossed and turned all night, and when she'd stumbled downstairs for some coffee, Ruth was already on her way out the door.

'Didn't want to wake you. Borrowed these,' she indicated the skirt and tee shirt. 'Hope you don't mind. Don't

forget to set the alarm after I've gone.'
She waved goodbye.

★   ★   ★

Marie wandered around the barn,
unable to settle or shake off a feeling of
unease. No matter the circumstances,
she shouldn't have let Jed drive off into
the night — supposing he had passed
out at the wheel and wound up in a
ditch — or worse?

There was always the possibility that
he had been telling the truth about
what happened and because she had
chosen to disbelieve him she had put
him in more danger.

Marie ran a hand through her hair.
What was it about Jed that stopped her
from thinking straight? No one in his or
her right mind could call him handsome. His smile was too lopsided, he
stuttered, and somewhere along the
lines his nose had come into contact
with a solid surface leaving it decidedly
off centre.

Apart from his lack of physical attributes there were so many gaps in everything else he told her, Marie didn't know what to believe any more. Even Ruth wasn't sure what he did for a living and she was a childhood friend.

In contrast Pierre was everything a girl could wish for — suave, cultured, good looking and charming. Why then didn't she feel the same way about him?

Marie decided it would do no harm to check up on Jed. She tried to convince herself it was for reasons of concern for his safety, but a small voice inside her head was telling her it was because she wanted to hear his voice again.

He had said he was going to spend the night with his sister. Marie didn't know her number — or Jed's either. In all the confusion she had misplaced the card he'd given her the first time they had met. That only left the contact number of Angela's legal team pinned up on the notice board. Marie dialled it. It was answered on the second ring.

'Hello, Tony speaking. How can I help you?'

'Er, I'm Marie Stanford, the niece of Madame Angela Dubois,' she began, wondering if she had been foolish beyond words.

'Maynard's barn isn't it? What can we do for you?'

'I was wondering if Jed Soames is in today?'

'Who?' The voice sounded blank.

'He's one of your security advisers? Actually I think he works from home but this is the only contact number I've got for him.'

'I've never heard of him. Hold on, I'll check. He might be one of our freelancers. I don't know them all.'

Tony was away from the line for quite a while. Marie tried to ignore her feelings of renewed suspicion. Had her first inklings of doubt been correct? Had Jed been lying to her all the time?

'Sorry it took me so long.' Tony was back on the line. 'System's playing up a bit today. Sure you've got the right name?' he asked.

'Yes, it's definitely Jed Soames.'

'Can't trace him. Of course I don't know how up to date our list is and the computer was down earlier on. Would you like to leave a message? If I do trace him I could contact him for you?'

'No, that's all right. Thank you for looking.' Marie replaced the receiver. She felt sick in the pit of her stomach. No wonder Jed had bolted last night. Her suspicions were getting too close to the truth for comfort. Ruth hadn't been holding back on her interrogation either. It wouldn't have taken the pair of them long to work out that his story about losing the keys was nothing more than a tissue of lies from start to finish.

There had been no prowler. Biddy must have disturbed him and he'd had to invent the first thing that came into his head, what a shock it must have been when she had insisted on telephoning for the police and an ambulance. No wonder Jed hadn't wanted to go to hospital. Marie bit her lip. All the same, there was no faking the bruise on his head. Could he have done that himself? And if so, why?

And why was everyone so interested in the keys to Maynard's? There was nothing of any value in the barn. Marie jerked up straight — except Angela's boxes! Both Jed and Pierre had seen them. Pierre had even moved the trunk, supposedly to gain access to the cloakroom and Jed too had been interested in their contents.

Had Angela managed to save some valuables from the fire and was she now claiming for them?

Was Angela involved in something she didn't want Marie to know about? And where did Pierre fit in? It was obvious that Jed and Pierre did not like each other. But had they met before? Picking up their body language, Marie didn't think so.

Someone ringing the front door bell drew her back to the present. Marie went to answer it, glad of the interruption.

'Billy?' Marie greeted the jockey standing on her doorstep.

'Not disturbing anything am I?' he asked with his usual cheerful smile.

'Come in. Sorry I didn't get a chance to say goodbye and thank you properly last night but there were so many people wanting a part of you and Ruth needed a prompt getaway.'

'Had a good time did you?' Billy asked.

'The best. Want some juice? I haven't had any breakfast yet.'

Billy raised his eyebrows. 'And I thought I was the late riser.'

He followed her through. 'Ruth tells me you had an incident out here when you got back.'

'Billy,' Marie poured out two glasses of orange juice, 'do you know Jed Soames?'

'I've met him once or twice. Why?'

'Do you know what he does for a living?'

'Um — insurance?' He didn't look too sure as he perched on a bar stool still smiling at her. 'I was only joking about him being a spy you know. Why do you ask?'

'No matter.' Marie popped some bread in the toaster. The fewer people who knew of her doubts about Jed the better. There were enough rumours flying around as it was. 'Is this a social call or are you selling more raffle tickets?'

'Bit of both really.' When Billy smiled a dimple dented his chin, making him look boyish and vulnerable. Marie could imagine the effect it would have on Ruth.

In the short time Marie had known her, she realised underneath the brusque exterior, her friend had a heart of gold and Marie knew Ruth's feelings for Billy ran deeper than she would ever admit.

'Ruth won the cuddly toy in the draw last night. I drove out to give it to her. It was a pink teddy bear.' Billy made a face. 'She wasn't best pleased.'

'I can imagine.'

'When I explained I hadn't been able

to fix the raffle for her to win the socket set she said I'd have to take her out for dinner to make up.'

'Good for Ruth. See you take her somewhere nice.'

'You mean somewhere that puts salt on the chips without you asking?' Billy enquired with an innocent look.

Marie laughed.

'You know, she thinks the world of you, Billy,' she said in a gentle voice.

'She means a lot to me too,' he said in an unusually serious voice. 'Now,' he straightened up, 'before I start getting all grown up, where's that juice?'

'You know you and Ruth are two of the best people in my life at the moment?'

'Now you're talking my language. I like being the best in someone's life. Actually,' Billy cleared his throat, 'I wanted to have a word with you privately, that's why I dropped in.'

'What about?'

'Pierre Dubois. I mean I know it's none of my business and all that.'

'What isn't?' Marie's interest quickened.

Billy paused. He seemed to have difficulty choosing the right words. 'Do you know where he is right now?'

'I'm not sure. He mentioned something about visiting some friends in Oxford. Why?'

'If I were you I wouldn't have too much to do with him.'

'Why not?'

'Let's say he lives above his means.'

'So do a lot of people.'

'With Pierre it's serious.'

'How do you know?'

'Word gets round. He moves with a fast international set. What's your relationship with him?'

'We're sort of cousins once removed by marriage, I suppose.'

'Word of advice,' Billy tapped the side of his nose. 'Keep it removed.'

'You're going to have to tell me a bit more than that, Billy,' Marie insisted.

He hesitated. 'Last year the charity held an anniversary ball. There was an auction to raise funds. I was the auctioneer.'

'Go on,' Marie prompted him.

'I'm not sure what happened. I mean we assumed the painting was genuine.'

'What painting?'

'The one Pierre donated. Anyway, the bids were high and the person who won paid a lot of money for the painting.'

'And?'

'It was a fake.'

'What?'

'I don't know the full details as I wasn't involved but the whole thing was very unpleasant and as you can imagine left a nasty taste in everyone's mouth. We couldn't do anything about it because Pierre hadn't actually said it was an original. We all assumed it was. Our mistake — but one we won't be making again, but it was for charity and the organisers weren't too happy about the matter.'

'I can imagine.'

'So, there you have it. I won't be mentioning the matter again.' Billy glanced at his watch. 'Better go. I've got to see a man about a dog and that's not an invented excuse. Been looking for a replacement for my dear old collie. She died last winter and I'm lost without her. There's someone out Stow way got a litter of puppies. Thanks for the juice. Take care.'

He kissed her on the cheek then whistled cheerfully as he made his way back down the drive towards his car.

★　★　★

Still feeling restless and in desperate need of fresh air after Billy had gone, Marie drove her car to the neighbour-ing village. The dry cleaners raised a few raised eyebrows at the state of the ball gowns then promised to have them ready for the next day.

Marie strolled out into the afternoon sunshine. It was too nice a day to work in a stuffy office and now she'd verified most of Ruth's accounts, there was very little to do until the end of the month.

Deciding she deserved a day off, Marie bought some fresh bread, cheese and cherries and drove out of the village into the surrounding countryside.

She parked the car in a quiet beauty spot overlooking the river valley and strolling through the local churchyard took several moments out to enjoy the 17th century architecture of the medieval spire. The soft grass of the graveyard swished around her legs. There was no one else about. The only sounds to break the silence were the rasp of a pheasant and the lowing of some cows in an adjacent meadow.

She could see down in the valley thatched cottages dotted the village, their golden stone mellow in the afternoon sun. Up here away from the hustle that had been her life, Marie could almost believe she had imagined the goings on of the previous few days.

She followed the footpath out of the churchyard until she came to a small clearing in the centre of which stood a large sun baked piece of sandstone. Settling down against it, she unwrapped her lunch and sipped some water, before nibbling on some cheese.

A bold robin swooped down on the remains of the bread roll Marie had discarded and pecked at the crumbs. She leaned back and closed her eyes.

She awoke with a start. The sun had moved over and the heat had gone from the day. Marie got to her feet and shook the remains of her picnic off her skirt. She glanced at her watch and realised in dismay she had been asleep for over two hours. The warmth of the day and lack of sleep last night had been too much for her.

Feeling refreshed she packed up her picnic and walked back to the car, grateful she passed no one on her way. She was sure her blouse looked a mess and her hands could do with a wash.

Marie wound down the car window before starting up the engine. It was too late to call in on Ruth now to see if she had Jed's sister's telephone number.

Thinking of Jed brought Marie back to harsh reality. She would have to email Angela and tell her about Pierre's visit and why the keys to the barn had been changed — twice.

Marie frowned. Something was nagging at the back of her mind. What was it that woman had said at the ball? The one who said she knew Angela from the old days — something about a face lift? Had Angela been scarred in the fire? Was that why she'd gone into hiding? Marie knew from personal experience scars of that nature took a long time to heal. She glanced at her arm.

★   ★   ★

The outside of Ruth's garage was deserted. Marie was grateful, there was no need to stop. Ruth's invitation to drop in had only been casual and Marie felt an inexplicable urge to get back to Maynard's.

As she drove carefully up towards Rush Wood she caught a flash of

170

movement beyond the trees. Was it Jed again? She held her breath, uncertain what she was going to say to him.

But the car parked outside Maynard's wasn't Jed's. It wasn't Pierre's either.

This one she didn't recognise, but as she drove up a tall elegant woman emerged. Although they had never met Marie would have recognised her anywhere from the photos they had exchanged.

It was Angela.

Pierre's True Colours
Shine Through

Pierre glanced at the newspaper, but the day's headlines failed to grab his attention. He had other more important issues to think about. As well as the coming transaction there was the matter of Racing Billy.

Bumping into Billy Hammond had been an unpleasant shock to Pierre, as well as a bit of a nuisance. He'd chosen the venue with care, a boutique hotel that catered for a discerning clientele.

Pierre had thought it was sufficiently out of the way for him not to meet anyone he knew. The last person he wanted to see was Billy Hammond striding down the footpath towards him. There had been no time to dodge out of the way and Billy wasn't an easy man to ignore.

'Pierre, what a surprise,' Billy had greeted him with a slap on the back, the sapphire eyes keen and enquiring, absorbing every detail of Pierre's business suit and his briefcase.

'Billy, Hello,' Pierre did his best to look pleased to see him. 'What are you doing here?'

'Buying a puppy. There's a man got a litter of them on the farm down the way. Are you interested in puppies too?'

'I regret puppies are not my scene.'

'No, I didn't think so.' Billy's smile was enquiring. 'So if you're not after a dog, what are you doing in this out of the way place?'

'Family matters,' Pierre answered with a smooth smile. 'In fact, I'm on my way to an important meeting now and I'm running late.' Pierre glanced at his watch, hoping to keep the conversation brief, 'So if you'll excuse me?'

But Billy proved difficult to pass.

'Actually, Pierre,' he began, 'I'm glad I bumped into you. I met a relative of yours last night.'

'Oh, yes?' Pierre did his best to keep his smile neutral.

'Marie Stanford — she's some sort of cousin, isn't she?'

'Yes.' Pierre shuffled uneasily on the footpath and again tried to pass Billy.

'Now let me get this right,' Billy smiled and made a gesture with his hands, 'your father married her mother's older half sister.'

'That is exact.'

'Hm. Thought so.'

'And now I really must be on my . . .'

'Yes,' Billy continued blithely, 'Marie came to one of our charity dinners with her friend, Ruth. Marie works for her, you see, does the figures. Lovely girl, isn't she? Her aunt's bought an old barn nearby and had it renovated. She's done a lovely job.' Billy's eyes looked unusually sharp as he said, 'but I suppose you know all this.'

'Well, er, yes.'

'Ruth tells me Marie's barnsitting until her aunt arrives.'

'Is that so?' Pierre began fiddling with his cuff links.

'Do you know, the poor girl, Marie, not Ruth, I mean has had two attempted break ins? She's only been here a short while. Is that unlucky or what?'

'Two break ins? Really? That is bad luck,' Pierre looked surprised, then added with a brief smile, 'I don't wish to sound impolite, I mean it's lovely talking to you, Billy, and we must meet up for a drink some time and catch up on all the news, but right now I have an important meeting. If you don't mind?'

'Bad business about that painting,' Billy still showed no sign of moving out of Pierre's way.

'What painting?' Pierre feigned casual interest.

'The one you put up for last year's charity auction.'

'What about it?' Pierre asked.

'Not a sound provenance, not an original.'

Pierre's eyes narrowed. 'I don't think I actually said it was.'

'No, you didn't,' Billy agreed with his usual charming smile, 'but it would have been polite to mention it was only a copy, don't you think?'

'If you say so,' Pierre agreed, anxious to cut Billy short. 'I'm sorry I'm going to . . . '

'Round here people don't like that sort of thing and,' Billy added, 'they have long memories.'

'Yes, well,' Pierre all but manhandled Billy out of his way, 'we'll talk about it another time, maybe. I hope to see you around some time. Must rush.'

Billy's polite smile didn't quite reach his eyes as he bid Pierre goodbye.

'Just thought you ought to know what folk are saying, au revoir,' he added as he watched Pierre hurry off up the footpath.

'And I'd give anything to know what you're up to now,' Billy muttered under his breath as Pierre disappeared into the grounds of the hotel.

He smiled to himself as the beginning of an idea began to take root.

That was the trouble with people like Billy, thought Pierre as he abandoned his newspaper. They were more astute than most people gave them credit for.

Pierre realised it had been a minor slip offering that copy painting for the auction. He should have mentioned its provenance to the organisers but he'd had a lot on his mind at the time. Of course as he hadn't actually passed it off as original they couldn't do anything about it, but for the sake of good practice the bidder should have been made aware of its origin.

Dismissing thoughts about Billy Hammond and his wretched auction, Pierre turned his mind to more pressing issues.

With so many people coming and going at Maynard's he wasn't finding it easy to gain access. If only that set of keys he had copied from the set in Angela's handbag had worked, he wouldn't be in this situation and if he had known about Marie actually being on the premises he wouldn't have even tried to use them.

Perhaps if he invited Marie out for a meal, he could persuade her to offer him coffee at Maynard's afterwards. How to talk Marie into opening up Angela's cases he wasn't sure, but Pierre wasn't naturally a negative person and he was sure he could come up with a reasonable explanation as to why he had to go through Angela's things.

Jed Soames was proving a nuisance too. Pierre had not counted on him having such a high profile. He would have to find some way to discredit him with Marie. Although if he read the situation correctly, Jed was doing quite a good job of that on his own and wouldn't need any help from Pierre.

Pierre made a gesture of distaste. This sort of thing was most unpleasant and would not have been necessary if Angela had seen sense and given him the miniatures in the first place. They had been in the Dubois family for years, and were always passed from father to son.

Technically they were his. If it hadn't been for that unfortunate misunderstanding he had had with his father over an unpaid bill Claud wouldn't have passed them over to Angela for safe keeping.

Pierre sighed. When Angela had first married Claud, Pierre had been little more than a child and lived with his mother. When his mother had also remarried and gone to America, Pierre had been taken in by his grandparents in Chamonix. It was only recently that he had really got to know Angela well, and it was obvious Claud was totally besotted with her.

That wretched fire was causing Pierre so many problems. He had tried to tell his father many times that the furnishings were dusty, old and a hazard that needed replacing. As for the wiring Pierre hadn't even dared to mention it. Claud had not listened. The only person he took any notice of was Angela.

'Pierre Dubois?'

Lost in his thoughts, Pierre had not noticed the dapper man approach his table.

'Mr Williams.' Pierre stood up to greet the new arrival and shook his hand.

'I'm pleased to meet you at last.'

'I've ordered some coffee to be served out here,' Pierre said. 'I thought it would be more pleasant to sit out on the terrace.'

'Thank you.'

The older man deposited his brief-case on the ground then sat down opposite Pierre on one of the wrought iron chairs.

'Do you have any news for me?' he asked after an exchange of pleasantries.

Pierre paused. 'I think so, yes,' he replied carefully.

'You sound doubtful.'

'No, everything is on schedule,' Pierre assured him.

'I have shown my client the photographs and he is interested in all twelve miniatures.'

'I understand,' Pierre nodded agreement. 'They are a rare and unusual example of early Italian renaissance work.'

'I would like to look at them and report back to my client. Do you have them with you now?'

'No,' Pierre made a gesture of apology. 'But I do hope to have them by the end of the week.'

Mr Williams frowned. 'My client is leaving for South America within the next few days.'

'That shouldn't be a problem,' Pierre replied smoothly, although his heart was racing. He consulted his lap top. 'I have a window in my diary at the weekend? Would that be convenient?'

Mr Williams nodded. 'Very well. After that I won't be able to guarantee the deal.'

The coffee arrived and Pierre used the diversion to extract some paperwork from his briefcase.

'Perhaps we should finalise the business side of the deal?' His smile sat easily on his tanned features now he was on firmer ground. 'Merci,' he said to the waitress, 'I will have mine black. Monsieur?' he looked across the table.

'As it comes,' Mr Williams replied.

Pierre's eyes returned from the waitress to the sound of laughter erupting from the bar.

'Lovely litter of collies,' he heard a voice saying. 'Had great difficulty choosing only one I liked. In the end I opted for a little lady with white socks and a black patch over one eye.'

'Monsieur Dubois?' He heard Mr Williams' voice coming at him as if from a great distance.

'So sorry,' he apologised smoothly, 'I was distracted by the noise from the bar.'

'Would you like me to close the double doors, sir?' the waitress asked as she finished serving the coffee. 'That way you won't be disturbed.'

'Yes. Thank you, that would be most kind of you.'

As she carried her empty tray back

through the bar and before she closed the doors Pierre caught sight of Billy sipping an orange juice. He looked up and raised his glass to Pierre before turning his attention back to his companions.

The Elusive Angela Arrives At Last

'Marie, darling. Hello.' Angela ran towards her niece, arms outstretched and scooped Marie up in a hug before Marie had a chance to get over the shock of finally coming face to face with her Aunt Angela.

'We meet at last. Let me look at you.' She held Marie at arms' length.

It was a slightly unnerving experience to be inspected by someone wearing a huge pair of dark glasses, but Angela had not taken them off, leaving Marie at a distinct disadvantage. She blinked into her own reflection facing her in the dark lenses, her smile of welcome hovering on her lips.

'You are so like your mother,' Angela hugged her again, 'only more beautiful. Why did we leave it so long? We should never have lost touch. I expect you've heard lots of dreadful stories about me, haven't you? Well, darling,' she gave a girlish giggle, 'I've come to tell you they're all true.'

She smelt of expensive perfume and the material of her leopard print dress tickled Marie's nose, making her sneeze.

'Bless you,' Angela said and they both laughed.

'I thought,' Marie sniffed as she tried to locate a tissue, 'you weren't joining us until the beginning of September.'

'I wasn't but my plans changed — again.' Angela hugged Marie again then stroked her hair away from her face to get a better look at her. She cupped a hand under Marie's chin. 'You don't know how good it is to see you. Come on,' Angela tugged at Marie's arm. 'Let's go inside and talk. Where have you been? I've been waiting in the car for ages. My keys wouldn't work in the lock.'

'No, I — er, had the locks changed.'

'You did?' Angela didn't pause for

breath and betrayed no surprise at this piece of news. 'I can't wait to get to grips with the garden. It's years since I've grown anything. What do you think of my interior décor? I haven't really had a chance to inspect it. Last time I was over here they'd done absolutely nothing. Have they made a good job of things?'

The questions tumbled from Angela's lips, not giving Marie a chance to reply. Laughing, she squeezed Marie's arm again.

'I am so excited, you don't know. I've been looking forward to this moment for ages. You've got two older brothers, haven't you? I'm longing to meet up with them, Sally and your father. This is absolutely the best day I've had in a long time.'

Angela did not stop talking as between them she and Marie managed to unlock the door to Maynard's and stagger through into the open plan living room. Angela collapsed in one of the chairs and took off her chic black beret. A mass of blonde curls tumbled down to her shoulders.

'Like it?' She ran a manicured hand through her hair. 'I had it done yesterday. Sorry, always talk too much when I'm nervous. Now,' she leaned forward, 'tell me absolutely everything. I want all the dirty details. What's been going on here?'

'It's difficult to know where to start,' Marie began, still trying to come to terms with this unexpected development.

'From the beginning, where else?' Angela laughed and leaned forward as though anxious not to miss a word.

'Well,' Marie looked round, 'this is it,' she said, indicating the living room. 'Maynard's barn.'

'I know that,' Angela wrinkled her nose.

'I arrived about two weeks ago.'

'I know that too. Tell me something I don't know,' Angela insisted.

Marie took a deep breath. Now was as good a time as any to break the bad news. 'Someone has tried to break in

— twice, I think.'

'My poor darling,' Angela gasped. 'Weren't you scared out of your wits?'

Marie dismissed the suggestion lightly. 'I was more annoyed than scared.'

'Have you any idea who it was?'

'No, and I don't know what they were after. Have you got anything of value in your packing cases, Angela?'

Angela paused then said, 'Not to my knowledge. I wanted to start again,' she said with a sad look on her face. 'There are only a few things from my past in my cases.' She looked round. 'Where are they?'

'I put them in the storeroom out of the way.'

Angela nodded. 'You can go through them if you like when you've got a spare moment. Would you be an angel and sort out the clothes for me? They'll be desperately creased.'

'Angela.' Marie was only half listening.

Angela jumped at the sound of her raised voice.

'Goodness, darling what on earth's the matter?'

'Do you know a Jed Soames?'

'I'm not sure. I may do. Why?'

'He was here the day I arrived. He was the one who discovered the first attempted break-in. He knew who I was from that photo I emailed you and he told me a story about being responsible for your security, but when I phoned up your legal people they'd never heard of him.'

'That sounds intriguing.' Angela didn't look in the least worried by this piece of information. 'Perhaps he's our mystery intruder. But why would he need to break in?'

'I don't know.' Marie chewed on her lower lip. 'Did you ask for special security?'

'No. I didn't see the need for it here. But you said something about a second break-in?'

'I went out one evening with Ruth Bradbury, she owns the local garage in the village . . . '

'She's the one you're working for?' Angela interrupted her.

'I do her accounts.'

'Clever girl,' Angela said, full of admiration. 'I must get you to try and sort out my finances. They are in the most tremendous muddle. Go on,' she urged Marie, 'don't stop halfway through.'

Marie frowned. It was difficult to concentrate on her story when Angela kept interrupting.

'We came back a bit early from the ball . . . '

'A ball?' Angela chipped in again, 'my, you do move in exalted circles.'

'Because Ruth had an early start the next morning,' Marie battled on determined not to be sidetracked further by Angela's interruptions, 'and we found Jed had been hanging around again. The police and an ambulance were here and he said he'd been attacked.'

Angela's blue eyes were wide with intrigue. 'And you didn't believe him?'

'I don't know. He had this huge

bump on his head and I suppose it did look real.' Marie sighed. 'But neither Ruth nor I could work out what he was doing here in the middle of the night. Jed insisted that he'd forgotten we were going out for the evening and that he'd only dropped by to deliver a spare set of house keys.'

'Well.' In one supple movement Angela stretched out her impossibly long legs. She reminded Marie of a sensuous cat. 'You do live in interesting times. Do you think this Jed was trying to break in?'

'I don't know. I don't think so and I can't see why he should want to, but the prowler, if there was one, couldn't have been Pierre, could it?'

'Pierre?' Angela stiffened and her smile was wiped off her face in an instant. 'Pierre's been here?'

'He was visiting friends in Oxford and dropped in to see you. He was very disappointed when I explained you weren't here and that I didn't know exactly where you were.'

'Pierre said that?' Angela's voice had lost all its earlier ebullience.

'Yes.'

'Where is Pierre now?' Underneath her glasses, Angela's face had gone pale.

'I don't know,' Marie admitted. 'Angela, is anything wrong?'

'Of course not,' she gave a shaky laugh, 'why should there be?'

'No reason. Anyway, you can speak to Pierre yourself. He's promised to take me out to dinner one evening.'

'When?'

'He said he'd call.'

Angela cleared her throat. 'I absolutely can't see him tonight if he calls, darling.'

'No, of course not,' Marie replied, unable to shake off the suspicion that something wasn't right between Angela and Pierre.

'I'm sorry to be a party pooper, my angel, but I am so tired and I can feel a migraine coming on. That's why I'm wearing these.' She indicated the dark glasses. 'I always get one when I'm stressed. There was a delay on the shuttle, then my hire car wasn't ready.' She stifled a yawn. 'Now all I want to do is sleep.'

'Your operation. Angela, I forgot. Have you been very ill?'

'I'm getting over it but I'm not up to socialising yet.'

'Do you want me to stay on now you're back? Or would you prefer me to leave you on your own?'

Marie was surprised to realise how disappointed she felt at the thought of leaving Maynard's barn. In the short time she'd been here she'd grown to love the sleepy village and her new friends.

'Darling, didn't I say? This is only a flying visit. I can only stay the one night.'

'But I thought . . . ' Marie blinked in bewilderment.

'I know you'll think me incredibly unreliable, darling,' Angela affected one of her light laughs, 'and I suppose I am, but I have to be back in London tomorrow. My agent wants to discuss photo shoots and the details of my new contract. That's why I dropped every-thing to come over at such short notice, but I'm not staying. I'll be in London for a few days then I have to go back to France. There is so much paperwork to see to, you cannot imagine.'

'Are you sure you don't want me to contact Pierre while you're here? He mentioned family matters too. He will have been so sorry to have missed you.'

'No.' Angela shook her head. 'He's bound to suggest we do all sorts of things I don't want to do. Let's have a girls' night in and get to know each other. I need to rest up if I'm going to be fit enough to drive back down to London in the morning. In fact, would you mind if I had a little rest right now? I mean I know it is appalling bad manners to fall asleep in front of a guest even if she is family, but I am almost dead on my legs.'

'I'll make your bed up.'

'I'll do it.' Angela stood up and had another stretch. 'Don't worry,' she smiled, 'I know the way. Would you bring me a cup of lemon tea in an hour or so?'

* * *

A loud ring on the door disturbed Marie. Lost in her thoughts about Angela, she had stayed on in the living room, trying to get her head round what had happened.

Jed was standing on the doorstep a hesitant smile on his face.

'Er — hello?' He looked uneasy. 'I've come to . . . '

'I'm so pleased to see you.' Marie dragged him through the door.

'You are?' He raised an eyebrow then gave her his crooked smile. 'There's a first.'

Marie glanced over her shoulder. 'Don't make a noise.' She held a finger to her lips in a gesture of silence.

'Why not?' Jed whispered back. 'Do

you want me to take my shoes off?'

'There's no need to whisper, but don't raise your voice and of course you can keep your shoes on.'

'That's good. Think I've got a hole in my socks.'

Marie took a quick step backwards away from Jed. Last night's parting words between them were too fresh in her memory, as was the feel of his body against hers.

'Angela's arrived.'

'Has she?' Jed looked suitably impressed. 'I wondered who the car outside belonged to.'

'She's got a headache and she is upstairs having a rest. She says she's not staying and she doesn't want to see Pierre if he calls.'

Jed made a noise of surprise at the back of his throat.

'Don't you see?' Forgetting all about keeping her voice down, Marie raised hers. 'Something is wrong,' she said.

'You don't think she's got a head-ache?'

'It's not that. I told her about you and . . . '

'I hope it was all good.' Jed didn't look in the least concerned by Marie's revelation. He seemed more interested in smiling at her. 'I haven't thanked you properly for rescuing me last night.'

'Jed, concentrate. Angela couldn't remember who you were.'

'That's probably because we've never met,' Jed pointed out. 'No, that's not true. We were once at the same party, but we weren't introduced.'

Marie looked hard at him. He blinked back at her. The bruise on his temple was still livid but looked less angry. Someone had cut away a section of his hair to treat it, and what was left was a spiky mess.

'Have I got a spot on the end of my nose or something?'

'No,' Marie said softly. 'You look ridiculous.'

'Well thank you very much,' he retaliated. 'That was my niece's handi-work if you must know. She insisted on tending to me. She wants to be a nurse when she grows up. She's got a long way to go,' he said with feeling, 'if that's the best she can do.'

'Were you really attacked?' Marie asked.

Jed grabbed Marie's hand. 'Do you want to feel the bump on my head? Ow,' he winced as her fingers came into contact with the wound. 'See? It's real all right. My sister's a dab hand with the witch hazel, but like her daughter, she's not very gentle. She took the worst out of it, but I'm not a hero and it still hurts.'

Marie snatched her hand out of Jed's. Every time he touched her it was as if someone passed an electric shock up her arm.

'By the way, I think,' he said slowly, 'we're making enough noise to wake ten Angelas.'

'What are you doing here anyway?' Marie demanded.

'I came to check up on you in my official capacity. Make sure you'd had 'no more midnight prowlers.'

'You're not a security guard are you?'

'Not exactly,' Jed admitted.

'Why is no one who they say they are round here?'

'You think you've got an Angela impersonator upstairs?' Jed enquired a look of surprise on his face.

'No, I don't. I know I'm not making sense, but everyone — you, Pierre and Angela, is hiding something from me.'

'What is Angela hiding from you?'

'She's wearing dark glasses.'

'Right.' It was obvious from the tone of Jed's voice that he didn't understand.

'She hasn't taken them off and she won't say what her operation was for. She's come over from France early and says she's not staying, and she doesn't want to see Pierre.'

Jed's voice was curiously soft. 'Anything else worrying you?'

'You are,' she said in challenge.

'Marie, I promise, you've no need to worry about me.'

She turned away from him not

wanting to hear any more stories. 'Then there's something Racing Billy said about not trusting Pierre.'

'Why are you worried about me?' Jed persisted, ignoring her remark about Pierre.

'Because,' she began slowly on a deep breath, 'you've been driving round with a bump the size of Wales on your head. I felt bad about turning you out into the night so I thought I'd check up on you, only I didn't have your number. I phoned the one on Angela's notice board. Her legal team have never heard of you.'

'That's because I don't work for them. I'm freelance. Didn't they explain?'

'They did say something like that,' Marie conceded.

'Well then?' Jed shrugged. 'What's not to believe?'

He drew her slowly into his arms. Marie offered no resistance. She could feel his heart beating against hers.

'I promise you I'm not your mystery housebreaker and that I am acting in

Angela's best interests. There, does that satisfy you?'

'How do I know I can believe you?' Marie asked, having difficulty catching her breath.

'Try this,' he murmured on a low breath.

The next moment Jed's lips were on hers. Marie could not stop herself responding to their gentle touch. His arms around her were firm and comforting and her body swayed against his. It was several moments before he released her.

'I've been wanting to do that for a long time,' he admitted with a wry smile, 'actually from the moment I frightened the wits out of you by jumping out of the bushes.'

'You have?' Marie replied in a hoarse rasp.

'Darlings, I hate to interrupt,' a bright voice behind Jed broke into the scenario, 'but we did say something about a cup of lemon tea and I am gasping.'

Jed took a long moment to look away from Marie.

'Hello,' Angela, who was still wearing her dark glasses, beamed at him. 'I hope your intentions towards my niece are honourable Mr, er, I don't think we've been introduced?'

'Soames,' Jed replied, not looking in the least abashed.

'So you're the mystery housebreaker. Darling,' Angela smiled at Marie, 'you didn't tell me he was quite so handsome. How do you do, Mr Soames.'

'Jed,' he said.

'Jed,' she replied, 'I'm Madame Dubois. Please do call me Angela.'

Angela Shows Her Uncertainty Over Pierre

'Wow,' Ruth stared open mouthed at Marie. 'You mean Angela turned up out of the blue with no warning?'

They were sitting in the back office of Bradbury's Garage sipping tea.

'She was waiting for me when I got back from my shopping. I was quite late because I had a picnic lunch, then I fell asleep in the sun. Sorry I didn't call in,' Marie apologised, 'but after I'd taken the ballgowns in for cleaning, I needed to chill out after all the excitement.'

'Understood, but why didn't you ring me?' Ruth demanded brushing aside Marie's explanation. 'You know I'm dying to meet up with her. I've heard so much about the famous Angela Dubois. Billy's been reading up on her. He's hoping to get her to help him with his charity work. She'll be a huge draw.'

'There wasn't time to ring you. She only stayed over the one night and she said she was tired. Then when Jed joined us . . .'

'Jed — what was he doing there?'

'He dropped by as well,' Marie rubbed at the burn scar on her arm in a nervous gesture of reaction, 'to check up on things.'

'Don't you mean you?' Ruth asked with a knowing look.

'He wanted to know if we'd had any more nocturnal visitors.'

It was another warm day and Marie knew her face was flushed. She had no intention of telling Ruth about Jed's kiss. Even now Marie couldn't quite believe it had actually happened.

After Angela had discovered them together, she had insisted Jed stay on for the rest of the evening, and far from looking exhausted, Angela had turned into the life and soul of the evening, regaling them with amusing stories from her art dealing days with Claud, to life on the modelling circuit.

They had heated up one of Sally's lasagnes that Marie had retrieved from the freezer and Angela had unearthed a bottle of wine from the boot of her car.

'House warming presents,' she had trilled as she began unloading a ripe Camembert and some juicy figs.

'And then she went off to London the next morning?' Ruth asked.

Marie nodded. 'She had an appointment with her agent to finalise her new advertising contract. She said if she had time she'd call in again before she went back to France, and there you have it.'

Ruth scratched her nose leaving a greasy smear on her face.

'What are you going to do now?'

'Angela wants me to stay on until September as we'd originally agreed. She wasn't sure of her exact plans as there are several matters needing her attention at the chateau and she's still convalescing.'

'Well, what a turn up for the books.'

Ruth bit into a ginger crunch. 'What's she like?'

'Very glamorous, chic, beautiful,' Marie raised her shoulders in a gesture of amusement, 'I can't believe she's my mother's sister. Mum is so ordinary. Actually she telephoned while Angela was there. They were on the phone for ages.'

'What about Jed?' Ruth asked.

'What about him?'

'Did Angela recognise him?'

'That's the strange thing,' Marie said, 'she didn't. Neither did it bother her in the least that he'd been hanging around Maynard's. Jed sort of brushed off my questions about security and Angela wasn't in the least bit interested in his back-story.'

'Well, if she's not worried, I shouldn't let it bother you. I've know Jed for years. He's totally honest. He wouldn't be involved in anything dodgy. Maybe there's a clause or something in her insurance that needed to be checked out. That seems the most logical explanation to me. He probably doesn't want to advertise the fact, so he told you he was involved in security. It's more or less the same thing.'

Marie so wanted to believe Ruth but she wasn't sure where her feelings for Jed were heading. If the explanation for his presence at Maynard's was as simple as Ruth suggested, why hadn't he said so?

'Yes, but then who attacked him?'

'Search me. What did you do all evening after you'd eaten your figs and lasagne?' Ruth too seemed to lose interest in the break ins.

'Angela and Jed talked about paintings. He's quite an expert on the Impressionists. He studied art at college. Did you know he lived in Paris for a while?'

'Might have done,' Ruth admitted. 'He was off the scene for a while in his teens.'

'He and Angela went on about brushwork and colour and how the politics of the day influenced the composition of art.'

'Pretty heavy stuff,' Ruth sympathised.

'So, there you have it.' Marie finished her tea.

Ruth looked faintly disappointed. 'There's no more?'

'That's it. Now I need to get down to some work.' She eyed the invoices unenthusiastically.

'And I've got a new set of tyres to fit.' Ruth jumped off the desk then paused. 'By the way, you haven't heard from Pierre have you?'

Marie shook her head. She was still baffled by Angela's reluctance to see her stepson and she hadn't lingered the morning after her arrival at Maynard's. Marie had waved her off immediately after breakfast. It was as if she couldn't get away fast enough.

'I don't suppose it means anything,' Ruth was standing in the doorway still hesitating.

'No more mysteries,' Marie said with a sigh, 'I've had my fill of things that don't add up.'

'There's probably nothing to it,' Ruth agreed, 'only Billy bumped into Pierre the other day.'

'Oh, yes?'

'Can't remember the name of the place, but it's down the road somewhere. There's a small hotel, all very exclusive and discreet.'

'Hardly Billy's scene I would have thought,' Marie commented with a smile.

'He'd been out looking at dogs.'

'A litter of farm collies? Did he get one?'

'How do you know about the collies?' Ruth frowned.

'He told me he was dog hunting when he called by the morning after the ball to see how I was. He'd heard from you about the trouble the night before.'

'Anyway, Billy bumped into him outside this hotel. It was obvious Pierre didn't want to be seen and Billy, being a bit on the inquisitive side, and with a score to settle with Pierre over that fake painting he landed him with at the auction, followed him inside at a discreet distance, and,' Ruth paused for effect, 'he saw him on the terrace with a man.'

'Ruth, where is all this leading?' Marie's hand hovered over the first of the invoices.

'Hang on. I'm getting to the interesting bit. Billy overheard Pierre and this man talking about miniatures. It sounded as though Pierre had got himself a deal. The other man had a client who was willing to make an offer, if Pierre could produce the goods.'

'And?'

'A deadline was mentioned.'

'Pierre did mention he was over here on business, perhaps that was it. He is a dealer, isn't he?'

'The thing is,' Ruth began to look a little uncomfortable.

'Out with it,' Marie said, 'then perhaps I can get on with some work.'

'I'm sure some early Italian miniatures were mentioned as missing in the reports of the fire at Claud's chateau.'

'How do you know?'

'I read about it in one of those glossy magazines. I was at the hairdressers having my hair put up for the ball and there was an article all about it. If we're talking about the same miniatures, they're supposed to be a family heirloom.'

'Are you saying these are the miniatures Pierre's trying to sell?'

'The point I'm really trying to make is we know Pierre is a bit short of cash. Those miniatures would get him out of trouble and if they were removed before the fire started, then they probably didn't go missing and are still in his possession.'

'Yes?' Marie agreed slowly.

'Supposing, and I know this is a long shot, but supposing they somehow got packed up with Angela's things.'

'Why?'

'I haven't worked that one out yet, but she has got some packing cases at Maynard's, hasn't she?'

Marie's brow cleared. 'You think

that's what the attempted break-ins were all about?'

'It's a theory. Perhaps. Pierre originally had some copy keys made that didn't work and then poor old Jed happened to be in the wrong place at the wrong time the other night and got bopped on the head.'

'Pierre did know Jed had a spare set of keys. He was there when Jed mentioned them.'

'There you are then. If it hadn't been for old Biddy walking her dog, interrupting Pierre, he might have used them to get into Maynard's. He knew we were out for the evening, didn't he?'

Marie nodded and then shook her head. 'It's not possible,' she dismissed the idea. 'If the miniatures are passed down from father to son, that means they belong to Pierre anyway. Technically I suppose he shouldn't be selling them on, but if he wants to, I suppose he can. And we still haven't worked out why he would put them in Angela's packing cases anyway.'

'Because he didn't want to be searched at Customs? They're a bit hot on that sort of thing, aren't they?'

'They could have searched through Angela's things.'

'That's just it. If they had done, she would get the blame, wouldn't she? Pierre could say he knew nothing about it.'

'Sounds a bit far fetched to me.'

'Do they get on?' Ruth asked, 'Pierre and Angela?'

'When I mentioned Pierre was in the area, Angela did go all tired on me and say she didn't want any visitors.'

'There you are then,' Ruth said with an excited smile. 'I think we've stumbled on to something.'

'Best keep it to yourself, Ruth,' Marie said. 'Angela asked me to go through her packing cases and sort out her clothes and get them laundered and aired. If I do a couple of hours here then go back home this afternoon, there's plenty of time to go through everything and look for miniatures.'

'Why don't you ask Jed to help you?'

Ruth's eyes lit up. 'If he's the expert you say he is, he'll be able to say whether or not they're genuine.'

★ ★ ★

When Jed had left Maynard's after their shared supper, Angela had discreetly made herself scarce while Jed said good-bye, but he hadn't kissed her again. In fact he hadn't made any plans at all to meet up. With no more than a brief wave, he'd strode off to his car, and driven away, without a backwards glance.

'You haven't got long to do it,' Ruth warned her.

'Marie hasn't got long to do what?'

Marie jumped at the sound of a voice behind Ruth, to where Pierre was standing, his eyes boring into Marie's.

'Have you been there long?' Ruth demanded.

'Long enough to hear what you were talking about.'

Pierre's smile did not quite reach his eyes.

The Truth About Jed Emerges

'Then you'll know we were talking about getting the invoices done won't you?'

Years of being in business had taught Ruth to think on her feet. She eyed up the stranger standing in the doorway behind her.

'I heard my name mentioned,' Pierre said.

'And who are you?'

'Ruth, this is Pierre,' Marie said quickly, adding, 'Angela's stepson.'

'Well, Pierre,' Ruth continued to address him, 'you know what they say about listeners never hearing any good of themselves?'

'And why were you talking about me?'

'Because you missed Angela's visit,' Marie replied.

The chocolate brown eyes narrowed. 'Angela has been here?' His interest quickened. 'I thought she was not arriving until September.'

'She had to come over for a meeting. She decided to drive up to Rush and see how I was settling in.'

'And how was Angela?'

'A bit tired. She said she had a headache.'

'She should be convalescing not driving around giving herself head-aches.' There was an angry slant to Pierre's mouth now.

'Well,' Ruth appraised him with eyes that were unusually cool, 'if you had been here you could have told her that yourself, couldn't you?'

Pierre ignored her. 'Is she coming back?' he asked Marie.

'I'm not sure.'

A silence fell between the three of them.

'Er,' Ruth broke into it, 'is there something we can do for you? If you need your car serviced I'm afraid you've come to the wrong place. I could get one of the lads to valet it for you if you like?'

'No. Thank you. I called in to see Marie. Please don't let me detain you.'

Ruth ignored the set down.

'Want me to stay, Marie? I could help with some of those invoices?'

'That won't be necessary but thanks.' Marie threw her a grateful look.

'In that case,' Ruth said glancing from Pierre to Marie, 'I'll be in the pit if you want me.'

She glanced over her shoulder as she closed the door behind her. The expression on her face left Marie in no doubt as to what she thought of Pierre Dubois.

Pierre shuffled towards Marie, frowning as piles of paperwork slid off a side desk.

'I should stay where you are,' Marie advised him, 'there's not enough room for two people to move about.'

Pierre's aftershave was overpowering in the confined space of the office and caught in the back of Marie's throat. She wished he would move out of her body space.

'I was on my way to Maynard's when I saw your car parked outside,' he explained. 'Will you be here long?'

'I don't know. Why?'

'I was thinking perhaps you would like to have dinner with me tonight?'

Marie attempted a confident smile. Pierre must not suspect she had other plans for the evening, plans that might seriously disrupt his.

'Sorry, there are some things I need to do this evening.'

'We could go out later if you like?' Pierre's smile did not slip.

'Perhaps another night?' Marie suggested tugging at the sleeve of her blouse. She didn't want Pierre to see her scar. He might interpret its heightened colour to nerves — and she was nervous. Ruth's revelations had seriously unsettled her. If Pierre was involved in anything underhand, she wanted nothing to do with it and she wouldn't know for sure, until she had inspected the contents of Angela's packing cases.

Her throat began to constrict. She hoped Pierre would accept her refusal.

'Tomorrow then?' he persisted. 'You cannot turn me down two nights running.'

'I think I'm going to have to. I'm not sure if Angela will be paying another visit to Maynard's,' Marie stalled. 'If she does, I've a few things I need to discuss with her.'

Pierre's lips tightened angrily. Marie realised he was a man who did not like to be thwarted. Outside one of Ruth's mechanics began to whistle and the sound broke the tension in the office.

'Now, if you'll excuse me I do need to get on, I've a lot to get through here and as you overheard Ruth say, I haven't got long to do it,' she added for good measure.

'It's a pity you can't find time to have dinner with me,' Pierre drawled. 'Are you sure I can't persuade you?'

'Why don't you give me a call next week and we'll see if we can fix something up?' Marie suggested.

She heard the roar of Pierre's powerful exhaust as he accelerated away from Bradbury's Garage after he strode out of the office. Letting out a big sigh of relief Marie went in search of Ruth. She was more than ever thankful that she had both sets of keys to Maynard's in her possession.

'Do you think you could keep one of these?' she said, dangling the spare fob in front of Ruth. 'I don't want Pierre getting his hands on them and as Jed lost the last lot, I'm reluctant to entrust them to him.'

'Sure.' Ruth clambered out of the pit. 'I'll hang them on the hook with all the other keys shall I in full view of everyone? They'll be perfectly safe. It's such an obvious place to put them, no one will think of looking for them there. What did he want?' Ruth gestured towards the smell of Pierre's exhaust fumes.

'To ask me out to dinner tonight.'

'Hoping I suppose that you would invite him back for a nightcap, so that he could somehow get you to open up Angela's cases?'

'We don't know that.'

'I would say we do. You did turn him down?'

Marie nodded. 'You wouldn't like to help me go through Angela's things would you?' she asked.

'I've got a date with Billy tonight.' Ruth didn't look Marie in the eye as she tried to clean her oily hands on an equally oily rag. 'We're going to collect his new collie.'

'Wish I was coming with you,' Marie admitted.

'You'd be very welcome,' Ruth offered.

'I'm not playing gooseberry to you two. I'll be all right going through Angela's things on my own.'

'What if the situation turns nasty? Pierre could come looking for you and there's no telling what someone like that will do when they're desperate. I'd be much happier in my mind if Jed collected you from here. I'll lend you Honey too if you like. She's a rotten guard dog, but she's got a bark like a Baskerville hound. Once she gets going, plaster falls off the walls.'

At the sound of her name, Honey lumbered over to Marie, tail wagging excitedly at the prospect of an outing.

Marie bent down to stroke Honey's silky coat. 'I can look after myself. I don't need Jed's help.'

'He's at his sister's, I think.' Ruth wasn't listening. 'I've got her number here somewhere. I'll give her a call.'

Marie knew she was beaten. If she carried on refusing Jed's help, she might arouse Ruth's suspicions.

'I'll do it in the office,' she mumbled and held out her hand for Jed's number. Any faint hope she had that Jed's sister might take the call was crushed when Jed answered on the second ring.

'Jed — it's Marie.'

'Something wrong?' His voice was whiplash sharp and sent a shiver down her spine.

'There've been some developments,' she began.

'Where are you?'

'I'm at Ruth's.'

'Want me to come over?'

'I should be through in about two hours, but if you're busy,' Marie began, already beginning to regret having made the phone call. She should be able to stand up to the likes of Pierre Dubois on her own. He was hardly likely to attack her and if she took up Ruth's offer of Honey as a guard dog, she would protect her.

'I'll be there.' Jed rang off before Marie could stop him.

* * *

Marie followed Jed's saloon down the lane leading to Maynard's barn. She had been signing off the last of Ruth's invoices when she'd heard his voice in

223

the garage. From what she could make out, Ruth was updating him on the situation and the need for urgency.

There was no one outside Maynard's as they drove up and Marie parked her car quickly and jumped out.

'Doesn't look like anyone's been here,' he said as he waited for her by the front door while Marie went through the complicated sequence needed to unlock the alarmed doors.

'Look, Jed, this was all Ruth's idea. You don't have to stay,' Marie began 'Honey . . . '

'Is currently snoozing outside Bradbury's Garage.'

Marie flicked back her hair and glared up at him. 'Aren't you taking rather a lot on yourself?'

'What do you mean?'

Marie wasn't sure. Seeing Jed again had only confused her feelings about him. Was he using her in order to get close to Angela? What was his interest in the miniatures? They were nothing to do with Angela's security, or her own.

'Right, now I am here,' Jed was displaying no trace of the tenderness he'd shown her on the night of Angela's impromptu dinner party, 'I suggest we make a start. Where are Angela's cases?'

'In the cloakroom, there are two of them and a trunk,' Marie indicated the door. 'I locked them up, to get them out of the way because Pierre fell over one of them the other day.'

'Want me to bring them through to the living room?'

'I'd better make an inventory for Angela,' Marie looked round for pen and paper. 'That way we won't misplace anything.'

'There's only one item I'm interested in.'

'Do you really think Pierre put the miniatures in Angela's luggage?' Marie asked.

'I don't know what to think, but if we do find them then both he and Angela could be implicated,' he replied.

'Angela's not involved in any fraud,' Marie retaliated, beginning to grow annoyed at Jed's high-handed attitude. 'She asked me to go through her cases. Would she have done that if she was hiding something?'

'Maybe not,' Jed agreed.

'And stop taking charge of things. You are here at my invitation, so why don't you act like a guest?'

Jed was busy undoing the fastenings on one of the cases and took no notice of Marie's protests.

'There were rumours about Claud's business affairs at the time of the fire and you could say it came at a very convenient time.' Jed's voice came at her from behind the back of a packing case.

'That's an outrageous thing to say.' Marie exploded. 'How can you mount a personal attack on Angela? You had dinner with her the other night.'

Jed looked up at Marie with eyes that bore into hers.

'You may as well know this now. You're bound to find out anyway, sooner or later.'

'Find out what?' Marie echoed, her heart thumping painfully in her chest.

'I'm not part of Angela's legal team.'

'I had already worked that out for myself.'

'I'm an insurance investigator.'

'A snooper?' Marie found it difficult not to sneer. 'I might have known.' How could she ever have thought Jed attractive? The man was a snake who'd wormed his way into her affections, in order to get to Angela.

Marie was pleased to see that by the tightening of his jaw her jibe had hit its target.

'Was part of your brief to seduce me?' she challenged him, her own anger rising.

Jed's face darkened. The bruise stood out on his forehead in angry hues of red and purple. 'Angela has submitted a substantial insurance claim. I have special responsibility for the works of art and all I'm saying is there are some irregularities.'

'Are you saying it's fraudulent?'

'I'm not saying anything. It's early days but we do need to know exactly what happened to the miniatures. They are listed as missing.'

'And you think Angela or Pierre set this whole thing up as some sort of scam?'

'It's possible.'

Marie's chest hurt as she tried to control her breathing. 'I suppose that's why you've been hanging around here, hoping to catch me out too? When you realised I wasn't involved you decided to resort to other tactics. Well, it may hurt your pride to know, your charms were lost on me.'

'Marie,' Jed's voice softened, 'I can understand how you feel.'

'No you can't.' By now she was so annoyed, if she'd had a suitable missile to hand, she would have thrown it at him. 'The other night you sat at that table, drinking Angela's wine and eating my mother's lasagne,' Marie pointed in the general direction of the breakfast bar, 'and you laughed and joked with

Angela, when all the time you were planning to stab her in the back. I call that the lowest of the low.' Her lip curled in disgust.

'That's not true.'

'All those things, those accusations you made about Pierre, they could all have been applied to you.'

'To the best of my knowledge I haven't accused Pierre of anything.'

'You led me to believe he was . . . '

'What?' Jed asked.

'You said he attacked you.' By now Marie was finding it difficult to think straight.

'I don't think I did, besides you accused me of inventing the whole affair if you remember rightly.' Jed's voice was now as tight as hers. 'It was only when I forced you to touch the bump on my head that you realised I might be telling the truth.'

'I want you to leave, now,' Marie tried to struggle to her feet, but Jed had already undone the first packing case and was busy unwrapping newspaper.

'Leave Angela's things alone,' she said. 'In her absence they are my responsibility and you don't have my permission to go through them.'

She watched Jed lift a package out of the case.

'What do we have here?' he asked in a soft voice.

'From the look of it I'd say you were unwrapping a vase,' Marie folded her arms. 'Are you now going to tell me that it's Ming Dynasty?'

'More likely Paris flea market,' Jed admitted. 'It's pretty but it's not worth much.'

He turned the vase over and inspected the base.

'Maybe not to you, but Angela must like it or she wouldn't have had it wrapped up and parcelled over here.'

'Actually I'm wrong.'

'Excuse me,' Marie raised her eyebrows, 'you make mistakes?'

Jed put his hand inside the neck and very slowly, very carefully extracted another newspaper wrapped package.

'What is it?'

Jed began to carefully unwrap the folds of newspaper. Nestling inside the final sheet on a bed of black velvet was a set of twelve Italian renaissance miniatures.

In a shocked haze Marie heard the telephone begin to ring in the kitchen. On legs that were numb, she rose to answer it.

'Miss Stanford?' A voice enquired, 'Miss Marie Stanford?'

'Yes?' Her voice was a hoarse rasp of shock, she cleared her throat. 'Marie Stanford speaking.'

'This is the police. I'm sorry to tell you your aunt's been involved in a car accident.'

'What?' Marie shrieked.

'Your name is in her passport as next of kin and . . . '

'Where is Angela? What's happened?'

She Has Always Mixed With
A Racy Crowd

'There's no doubt about it, they're genuine.' Jed looked across the desk to the man seated opposite him.

'Then they are Italian Renaissance?'

'Yes.' Mr Smithers nodded. 'But the strange thing about them is,' he continued with a professional smile, 'although they are genuine, they are actually not as valuable as one would think.'

'They're not?' Jed's interest quickened.

'They have a rarity value of course and might fetch a reasonable price at auction, but we're not talking big ticket. This sort of thing was very popular at one time, but they are only family portraits and the sitters are not anyone of note.'

'I see,' Jed frowned. 'So what you're

saying is it would hardly be worthwhile making a false claim for them?'

'That's more your area of expertise than mine,' Mr Smithers replied, 'but let's say if you're going to get involved in that sort of activity, you could do better.'

'I understand.' Jed folded the miniatures back into their velvet pouch. 'You've been most helpful, Mr Smithers.' He stood up. 'Thank you for your time.'

'My pleasure,' he replied. 'Would it be indiscreet of me to ask if this is any way involved with the fire at the Chateau St Georges?'

'There is a connection,' Jed admitted.

'I thought I recognised them. Those particular miniatures have been in the Dubois family for years. Claud Dubois never had much sentimental attachment to them. He was more interested in encouraging new talent, and I believe some of his purchases have turned out to be wise investments. I do hope none of his modern collection was damaged in the fire.'

'The claim is still under investigation. I can't say any more.'

'Of course not.' Mr Smithers nodded, 'for what it's worth, I had a few professional dealings with Monsieur Dubois and I have to say I always found him a man of the highest integrity. His death was a great loss to the art world.'

* * *

Outside a fine drizzle of rain misted the atmosphere, leaving the pavements refreshed after the searing heat of the past few weeks. Jed took a deep breath enjoying the feel of moisture on his skin. He needed the sensation to clear his head and to help ease the throbbing of his aching bruise.

He had not heard from Marie since she had rushed off after the phone call about Angela leaving him clutching the miniatures and standing in the middle of the living room surrounded by rolls of scrunched up newspaper and empty packing cases.

When Marie's mother had rung moments later, Jed had been at a loss to know what to say.

'I've had the police on the telephone wanting to speak to Marie.' She had hardly given him time to pick up the receiver.

'Yes, they called here a few moments ago.'

'They found my daughter's details in Angela's passport.' Sally was breathless from speaking so quickly. 'Who are you?' she demanded.

'My name is Jed Soames. I'm a friend of Marie's. We were going through Angela's things, getting them out of their packing cases for her, when the call came through.'

'I see.' Sally sounded mollified. 'Sorry to sound so tense. I'm not thinking straight. As I understand it Angela's been involved in a car accident. Do you know if she's badly injured?'

'I'm sorry, Mrs Stanford, I don't,' Jed apologised. 'All I can tell you is it happened on one of the side roads after she left the motorway. We think she was on her way back up here from London. She said she would try to come back if she could. Marie's gone to find out exactly what happened.'

'My poor sister.' Sally's voice was now full of sympathy. 'She's had so much to put up with this year, first the fire, then losing Claud, then an operation — and now this. What was that, dear?' Jed heard her call out. 'I'm trying to find out. Sorry,' she apologised to Jed. 'My husband's in a bit of a state too. Angela always did lead an adventurous life. I wish now I hadn't persuaded Marie to house sit for her. It seemed like a good idea at the time. Who did you say you are again?' Sally sounded distracted.

'Jed Soames, I'm an insurance investigator.'

'Insurance investigator?' Sally's voice was now a shriek. 'You're not investigating Angela, are you? I do hope I haven't got Marie involved in anything unsavoury.'

'Not at all.' Jed did his best to reassure Marie's mother. There was no point in worrying her with details about break ins and lost keys.

'I mean, I'm sure Angela is honest,' Sally didn't sound to certain, 'but she has always mixed with a racy crowd.'

'Mrs Stanford,' Jed began, 'do you know anything about Pierre Dubois?'

'Who?'

From the quickness of her reply Jed didn't doubt Sally had never heard of him.

'Is he something to do with Angela? I'm afraid I can't help you much with her personal life. We've only recently re-established contact.'

'No matter,' Jed replied.

'Angela managed to trace us through some old mutual friends I believe but before that we hadn't heard from her for years. You know what it's like. It's something at the back of your mind that you always meant to do but you never get round to. Angela got in touch first. Sorry, I'm rambling, aren't I? You will tell my daughter to contact me as soon as she can, won't you?'

'Immediately she gets back.'

'I had a feeling Marie was hiding something from me. Call it a mother's instinct but I knew things weren't right.' She hesitated then said, 'You will look after her, won't you?'

'I'll do my best,' Jed said with a wry smile. He wasn't sure exactly where he stood on that score and he had a niggling suspicion that looking after was the last thing Marie needed from him, but that was something else Marie's mother didn't need to know. 'Try not to worry, Mrs Stanford,' Jed reassured her. 'I'm sure things will work out.'

'I hope you're right.' Sally did not sound convinced.

★　★　★

Jed strode along the main street fronting the art gallery, mulling things over in his mind.

Until Mrs Stanford's phone call, he hadn't been too sure about Marie's involvement with Pierre. At every opportunity she had stood up for Pierre, accepting his word against Jed's, but from what her mother had said, the arrangements made for Marie to house sit at Maynard's appeared to have been very last minute.

Passers-by glanced in his direction. His white T-shirt was soaked to his skin. People were struggling with umbrellas, difficult to unfurl after such a long dry spell but Jed hardly noticed the rain as it plastered his hair to his forehead.

Ever since he'd met Marie his thoughts had been in turmoil. He hadn't liked misleading her as to the true nature of his occupation but assessors often had to work under cover and it was a habit he found difficult to shake off. The story about him being Angela's bodyguard had gained momentum and Jed hadn't known how to stem it.

Most jobs of this nature were routine.

Ordinary people like Angela, confused over exactly what had been lost in house fires or floods, often made mistakes. It was natural and Jed believed Angela's error over the miniatures was genuine. He hadn't bargained on Angela's niece being such a beautiful, uncomplicated, plucky girl who didn't shy away from staying in a barn in the middle of a wood, even though she knew there were spare keys flying about all over the place.

Losing the spare set had been unbelievably careless of Jed but Marie hadn't once laid the blame for their loss at his door. He still wasn't too sure exactly what had happened that night in the wood. He couldn't shake off the sneaking suspicion that he'd lost his footing in the mud as he'd got out of the car and falling, had banged his head on the door. The lurker, whoever he was, must have seized his chance and grabbed his briefcase, with the keys in it.

Jed didn't blame Marie for mistrusting him after all the stories he'd told her. He had hoped to reconnoitre Maynard's that night, in case there was a further attempted break in, but all he'd managed to do was draw attention to himself in a way that would have disgraced an amateur.

And now, unprofessional though it may be, he realised he had fallen in love with Marie, a girl who didn't believe a word he said.

'Yoo hoo,' a voice interrupted his thoughts.

He looked up to see Ruth Bradbury strolling towards him, arm in arm with a jaunty man whose face seemed familiar.

'Jed?' she greeted him with a beaming smile. 'Want you to be the first to know.' She held up her left hand. On the third finger a solitaire diamond sparkled back at him. 'We've just been to collect the ring. We're engaged.'

'I couldn't keep running away from her forever,' the man standing beside her joked, 'she's one determined lady.'

Ruth nudged him playfully. 'You were

the one who said we'd make a good team and, liberated female though I am, you actually did the asking, I seem to recall.'

'Spare my blushes, please.' Her partner cast a desperate glance in Jed's direction.

'Congratulations,' he said, surprise driving all other thoughts from his mind. He glanced at Ruth's companion.

'You've met Billy, haven't you?' She made the introductions, 'Billy, this is Jed Soames. He's a friend of Marie's and I'm an old friend of his sister's.'

The two men shook hands.

'I was at your charity auction last year,' Jed said.

A shadow crossed Billy's face at the mention of the auction, but before he could say anything, Ruth butted in, 'What's all this about Angela being in an accident last night?' she asked. 'Marie left a garbled message on my answer phone this morning. Billy and I found it when we got back from the farm.'

'I know as much as you,' Jed replied with a troubled frown. 'Marie and I were unpacking Angela's things when she received a telephone call from the police.'

'The police?' Ruth raised her voice in concern.

'I'm hoping it was only routine. Marie is listed as next of kin in this country and her details were in Angela's passport.'

Ruth shook her head slowly. 'Whatever next? Ever since Angela Dubois purchased Maynard's, life has been a constant round of excitement and intrigue.'

'Marie's mother said the same thing,' Jed agreed, 'she telephoned Maynard's after Marie left because the police had been in touch with her as well.'

'Did you find the miniatures?' Ruth demanded.

'Yes,' Jed said slowly.

'I've no idea what either of you are talking about,' Billy complained, 'but if you want my opinion, it is possible

Pierre is involved with trying to sell them on. I overheard him discussing them with a dealer.'

'Well, he's in for a shock,' Jed replied. 'I've just been informed by an expert that while they are a very desirable example of their art, they are technically not worth much.'

'Hah, that'll teach him,' Ruth crowed. 'Do you know he marched into my garage the other day as though he owned the place and then treated me like the hired help? I soon put him in his place, I can tell you.'

The two men exchanged wry looks.

'By the way,' Ruth gasped in excitement, 'I forgot to tell you, there's been so much going on. I've had Biddy from the bakery call in. You remember? She was walking her dog in Rush Wood the other night? Well,' Ruth had hardly paused for breath, 'she's got your briefcase.'

'What?' Jed exploded.

'Seems her dog ran off with it.' Ruth began to laugh. 'She didn't realise until she got home. That's why she rushed off after the police arrived you see, because her dog had disappeared. Anyway it wasn't until the next morning she found it in the bushes outside her bungalow. I've got it at the garage if you want it. It's a bit muddy, but as far as I can see it's all intact.'

'You mean there wasn't a break in after all?' Billy asked looking puzzled. 'You banged your own head?' he peered at Jed's bruise. 'You made a good job of it if I may say so.'

'I, er,' Jed cleared his throat, 'I'm not sure what happened.' He admitted. 'The whole thing is rather a blur.'

'Looks like Pierre's in the clear anyway,' Ruth said, then tugged Billy's arm. 'We should be getting back. I've a customer booked to collect her car later this afternoon.'

'Can we give you a lift?' Billy asked Jed. 'You're soaked through.'

Jed shook his head. He was still trying to come to terms with Ruth's revelation.

'I'll soon dry out and I've a report to

compile. I'll do it in the library. It's quieter there than at my sister's house and thanks for looking after the briefcase, Ruth. I'll call in and collect it.'

'Any time. Keep in touch if you hear anything, won't you?' she waved goodbye.

★　★　★

It took Jed most of the afternoon to draft out his report for the assessors. High profile claims, such as this one, required delicate handling and Jed wanted to be sure he got his details right.

The dubious reports about Claud's business affairs were only hearsay, what the management needed was facts. Now he knew the second attempted break in was nothing but an unfortunate accident, he was pleased he could dismiss Pierre from his enquiries.

It was late in the afternoon before Jed finished his notes. He checked his mobile. He had missed only one message — from Ruth.

The recent shower had brought down

some early autumn leaves. Jed was careful not to slip on the path outside the library as he stood under the awning to call Ruth back. His bruise wasn't quite so angry now, but he had no wish to have another accident.

'Jed, thank goodness.' Ruth sounded relieved to hear his voice. 'Your sister gave me your mobile number. Did Marie leave you with her keys to Maynard's last night?'

'Yes, she dashed out and told me to lock up. Said you had a spare set she could use to get back in. Why?'

'Jed, I need you to go up to Maynard's, now. While Billy and I were out this morning I left a mechanic in charge of the workshop.' Ruth paused. 'I don't know how to tell you this.'

'What is it? What's happened?'

'Pierre called by, I suppose on the off chance of seeing Marie.'

'And?'

'When Marie left her spare keys with me, I put them on the board outside the office. I thought if they were in full view no-one would take any notice of them. They were just another set of keys. Pierre must have recognised them. The mechanic said he was distracted by the puppy, that's when it must have happened.'

'When what must have happened?' Jed demanded through gritted teeth.

'It wasn't until after I'd been back some time that I realised. There was quite a lot of work to do on that service I mentioned and . . .'

'Ruth.' Jed's voice startled some starlings. They flapped out of the trees at the sound of his raised voice. 'What happened?'

'The keys to Maynard's are missing. Pierre must have taken them.'

'I'm on my way,' Jed said.

Striding back to where he'd parked his car he threw his briefcase into the back and wrenched open the driver's door. Gunning his car into life he accelerated out of the car park leaving behind him a smell of burnt rubber on the wet tarmac.

I Can Tell He's In Love With You

'Darling, honestly, it's not as bad as it looks. There was absolutely no need for you to drive all the way down here, much as I appreciate the gesture.'

Marie stood at the end of Angela's bed looking down at the rather frail figure of her aunt. Her face was as pale as the bed linen and despite her protestations there were dark circles under her eyes.

'But your eyes are bruised,' Marie protested.

'You look exhausted too. Sit down.' Angela insisted, indicating a bedside chair.

Marie swayed on to it.

Angela frowned at her. 'What have you been doing to yourself?'

'The main road was closed last night. I couldn't get through,' Marie's voice caught in her throat. 'I thought it was because of your accident.'

'My poor darling, what a shock for you. I didn't close any road. My accident was only a minor bump.'

'Didn't you hit your head on the steering wheel?'

'Never mind about all that.' Angela flapped her hands as Marie tried unsuccessfully to stifle a yawn. 'Didn't you get any sleep last night?'

'I spent what was left of it in my car.'

'What on earth . . . ' Angela ran out of words.

'I wanted to be the first to get through when the road reopened. When the police called Maynard's, I thought, I thought . . . ' Marie shook her head. 'I don't know what I thought. All I do know is I had to see you.'

'How can I ever make things up to you? Darling, I'm so sorry. This is all my fault.'

'What were you doing haring round the countryside anyway?' Marie demanded.

'I was driving back to Maynard's

because I felt I owed you an explanation about everything that's been going on in my life.'

If Angela hadn't looked so pale, Marie would have shaken her. Her own head was aching from lack of sleep and her eyes were gritty with tiredness. For the first time she could sympathise with her grandfather and understand why he had thrown Angela out of the house.

She'd managed to refresh herself briefly in the hospital shower room before she'd been allowed to visit Angela. The nursing sister had informed Marie that Angela's injuries were superficial but the sight of her bruised face didn't convince her niece.

'I've never been a very good driver,' Angela confessed, 'and I'm not used to driving on the left. I suppose I wasn't concentrating when I swung out of that side road. Luckily I missed a poor cyclist coming the other way, but I wound up in the hedge.'

'Did you do any damage?'

'The hedge won't sue but I don't

think the hire car company will be too happy with me. Sorry, darling,' Angela made another gesture with her hands, 'you're tired and fed up and I'm cracking silly jokes. Honestly, apart from a few cuts and bruises, I'm fine. You must let me pay for a hotel room for you tonight. Where's my handbag?' Angela reached out to her cubicle.

'I don't want a hotel room,' Marie insisted. 'I want to know about you. What have you done to your eyes?'

It was the first time Marie had seen Angela without her dark glasses. Her brilliant blue eyes were pink and watery.

Angela sipped some water. 'I have a confession to make, darling. The bruises are nothing to do with the accident.'

'What then? Did you fall down the stairs?'

'No. Nothing like that.' Angela paused before admitting, 'I've had minor cosmetic surgery.'

'What?' All trace of tiredness left Marie.

'It's a long story, darling, but I was so desperate to get this make up contract that I succumbed. It was nothing too drastic just a little tidying up. You see there were several other models on the shortlist for the promotion and to be honest they are all stunning. One of them is the producer's girlfriend, so you can imagine the competition was pretty fierce. The camera can be very unforgiving to a more mature skin, so I thought I needed a little help.'

'Honestly, Angela. I could throttle you,' Marie protested. 'Don't you realise you don't need surgery? You're beautiful.'

Years of high living had in no way impaired Angela's beauty. Pale as she was, there was no denying her skin still held the dewy softness of a much younger woman, her dazzling smile and cheekbones did the rest.

'Any make up company would be mad not to sign you up immediately.'

'Darling, that's sweet of you to say so,' Angela patted Marie's hand, 'but my mirror tells me the traumas of this past year have left me looking slightly the worse for wear.' She gave a sad smile. 'And my beloved Claud's left his affairs in something of a mess, so not only did I need the operation to get the contract, I needed the deal to pay a few bills.'

'You should have told us. The family would have rallied round and helped out.'

'I was going to tell you that evening at Maynard's, but when your lovely boyfriend descended on us I could hardly bring it into the conversation, could I? So I kept my dark glasses on and pretended I had a migraine.' Angela made a face.

'Why didn't you tell me or Mum what you were planning to do?'

'Because you would have tried to bully me out of it,' Angela replied.

'Too right we would.'

'That's just it, darling. I've never been good at confrontation. I would have given in, then,' Angela shrugged, 'if I hadn't been offered the contract perhaps I would have blamed you and that would have been the end of our grand family reunion.'

Marie was struck by a sudden thought. 'If you were so keen not to tell us what you were up to why did you leave your convalescent home?'

'Because my agent needed me to firm up on a few last minute details. Contracts had to be signed and a forty-eight hour deadline was imposed so I had no choice. Of course once I was in the old country I couldn't resist driving up to The Cotswolds to see how you were getting on at Maynard's.'

'You should have let Mum look after you, she's brilliant at that sort of thing.'

Angela blinked rapidly to clear her eyes. 'Tears are supposed to be a good cleanser,' she tried to turn her expression into a smile. 'Can you imagine what your father would have to say about a neurotic woman being foisted on him?'

Marie had a pretty good idea, but she

let the question pass. 'You're not neurotic,' she felt duty bound to protest.

'You haven't seen me on a bad day,' Angela joked.

'And Dad wouldn't have minded,' Marie insisted. Once the dust had settled she knew her father really wouldn't mind. He never minded anything the family did.

'I expect your mother would have talked him round but there's not much room in their bungalow, is there? After a week of my company, your poor father would have been climbing the walls. I'm not the easiest person in the world to live with, darling. I never have been. You know Sally's father washed his hands of me? What that poor man went through I dread to think.'

'That was all a long time ago.' Marie's lips softened into a gentle smile. 'You know you won't half get it when Mum hears about this.'

'You're not going to tell her?' Angela looked like a teenager caught smoking behind the bike sheds.

'She'll find out. She always does,' Marie informed her.

Angela made a face. 'Silly to be scared of your younger sister, isn't it?'

'You've every reason to be. Mum can be quite fierce when she's roused.'

'In a way it will be nice. I've always been the sort of person who needs someone to look after them. I've never had anyone care about me before.'

'You had Claud.'

'He was my husband and I loved him dearly, but Sally's my sister. She's family and families say things to each other that a husband wouldn't. Am I making sense?' Angela stifled a yawn. 'I've been pumped full of so much stuff I'm feeling groggy.'

'Would you like me to leave?'

'After all the trouble my agent's gone to, to get me a private room? No way,' Angela shook her head and then winced. 'Ouch, mustn't do that too often.'

'What will you do now?' Marie asked.

'Will you be going back to France?'

'My ticket's rebooked for the day after tomorrow.'

'Are you fit enough to travel?'

'I'll be fine,' Angela assured her. 'I've got things to sort out at the chateau,' she paused. 'You heard about the fire?'

'Jed told me.'

'It was in all the French newspapers because Claud was quite well known.'

'You don't have to talk about it,' Marie put a hand over Angela's. 'It must have been a very distressing time.'

'It was.' Angela nodded. 'Of course the fire was a complete accident. Something to do with faulty wiring, but the insurance company is being very difficult and won't settle. The trouble is I don't know exactly which paintings were in the chateau, so my claim is not totally accurate. I told them Claud ran that side of things, and any records he made were burnt in the fire.'

'There's something I've got to tell you,' Marie said.

'Not more bad news, darling?'

Angela's eyes widened.

'I only found out myself yesterday. Jed is an insurance investigator.'

'Your lovely boyfriend?' Angela looked shocked.

'He is not my boyfriend,' Marie spoke through gritted teeth.

'No?' Angela did not look convinced. 'So why were you locked in a passionate embrace the first time I met him?'

'That was . . . '

'Yes?'

'Unfortunate.' Marie knew she sounded unconvincing, but it was the only word she could think of to describe the situation.

'I won't tease you,' Angela took one look at her heightened colour and patted her hand. 'So, your Jed, sorry I mean Jed, is investigating me? He won't find anything in my packing cases.'

'He already has.'

'What?'

'A set of Italian Renaissance miniatures.'

'Those old things?'

'Jed said they were reported as missing.'

'They could have been,' Angela shrugged, 'but does it matter? They are not worth anything.'

'Pierre seems to think they are.'

A shadow crossed over Angela's face. 'Then he's welcome to them. Technically they are his anyway, not mine.'

'Then why aren't they in his possession? Why did you smuggle them over?'

'I didn't.' Angela's voice rose in indignation. 'Claud gave them to me for safekeeping but to be honest I forgot all about them. Where exactly did you find them?'

'Stuffed inside an old vase.'

'You can give them to Pierre if you like. I don't want them.'

'Jed's got them. He was going to have them valued.'

'As you wish.' Angela plucked at the hospital sheet distractedly.

'What's the matter?' Marie asked. 'Is there something between you and

Pierre that I don't know about?'

Angela pondered for a few moments before nodding. 'When did you first meet him?'

'About two weeks ago. Why?'

'And he said he thought I would be at Maynard's?'

'Yes.'

'He was lying to you.'

'What?'

'He came to visit me at my convalescent home after my operation. I had stipulated no visitors but he must have used his charm on the staff. Unfortunately he was listed as my next of kin so he had every right to see me, but I didn't want to see him.'

'Don't you get on?'

'It's not that.' Angela sighed. 'I didn't want anyone knowing the exact nature of my operation.'

'Why would it matter if Pierre had known about your eyes?'

'Pierre is always short of money.'

'Is that why he's doing a deal with the miniatures?'

'Is he? Probably,' Angela nodded. 'He's not too particular how he gets his money. The thing is Pierre is very charming and as long as I don't see him too often, I love him to bits, but,' Angela hesitated again, 'he has friends in the media, friends who would pay well for the story that the celebrated Angela Dubois is having a facelift.'

'A facelift?'

'They always exaggerate these things and there is no way I could refute the story. It would mean going to court, all at horrendous expense, and the only winners would be the lawyers.'

'So you thought you would stay out of his way until the scars had healed?'

'Yes.'

'Would it matter terribly if Pierre did sell his story to the tabloids?' Marie asked. 'It would mean publicity for your campaign.'

'This would not be the sort of publicity they are looking for, darling. You see the range of cosmetics I will be promoting is to be aimed at the older woman who wants to look her best. I am an older woman and the slant they will be taking is that my looks are wholly natural and if ladies of a certain age use the products . . . '

'They'll want to look like you.'

Angela nodded. 'I haven't contravened the terms of my contract, or anything like that and my agent had full knowledge of my operation. It really was very minor surgery, but it could jeopardise the launch if Pierre was, well indiscreet.'

'Do you think he suspects?' Marie asked.

'I'm not sure. If he makes enough money on the sale of these miniatures he may forget about the whole thing. He'll come up with another money-making scheme I don't doubt. He's been trying to run some sort of art school where people copy famous paintings, I don't know how successful it was.'

'He used to keep all his stuff in an old outhouse at the chateau. He thought Claud and I didn't know about it, but we did. I heard from the caretaker that he's been back to collect all his stuff. I expect he wanted to cover his tracks in case people started nosing around.' Angela laughed. 'As if I care what he gets up to in his silly shed.'

'Billy Hammond, Ruth's friend, landed up with one of his paintings at a local auction. I think the successful bidder thought it was genuine.'

'That's what I mean. Pierre doesn't actually do anything against the law, but he's not entirely — honourable?'

'Billy overheard him doing a deal with some man who had a client who sounded interested in the miniatures.'

'Then you must give them to him,' Angela insisted. 'I will not have him frightening you and trying to gain access to my property for such a stupid reason. I suspected he copied my keys that day he visited me at the convalescent home. It's all so stupid. I would have given them to Pierre if he'd asked for them.'

'Claud only entrusted them to me because he and Pierre had some silly falling out. I didn't even know what it was about. It was always happening. The reason I kept Claud and Pierre apart was because petty squabbles distressed Claud. I think Pierre suspected me of trying to come between them, but it wasn't like that. The doctor said any excitement was bad for Claud, with his heart condition, so I made sure he wasn't excited.'

'You'd better scribble down some sort of authority saying he can have the miniatures and when I next see Pierre I'll give them to him.'

'Darling, how sensible,' Angela said, 'I can see you are going to be an invaluable ally. With you and your mother to look after me I shall be so happy.'

Marie stood up. She was beginning to wonder what they had let themselves in for.

'I'd really better go and leave you to have a sleep.' She leaned forward and kissed Angela on the forehead. 'Promise me you'll behave in future?'

'I'll try, darling, but no one's ever stopped me from doing exactly what I've always wanted.'

'I can believe it,' Marie answered with a wry smile.

'Darling,' Angela's voice was drowsy.

'What?'

'One more thing. Jed Soames.'

Marie stiffened but Angela didn't notice. 'I've known lots of men in my life.'

'Angela,' Marie said, 'get some rest. This can wait for another time.'

'What I'm trying to say is,' Angela's voice was now a sleepy murmur, 'Jed's a winner. Stick with him. I know a lot about men and I can tell he's in love with you. You'd be mad to let him slip through your fingers.'

Marie Resolves Her Problems
With Pierre

The light was fading from the day before Marie finally left the hospital. The site shop had provided an emergency kit of bathroom necessities for Angela, and Marie also bought her a hairbrush and a fashion magazine to browse. Then the smell of coffee lured her into the next-door café. It had been hours since she had eaten anything and the sight of a golden cheese topped pizza was a temptation she could not resist.

Notices posted around the public area requested that all mobile telephones be switched off. Marie was pleased that the ban stopped her from checking her voicemail. She sipped her cappuccino and took a few moments to unwind.

The ward sister had assured Marie that Angela's injuries were superficial and that she was only being kept in overnight for a check up. She knew nothing about any police follow up to the accident and as soon as she wanted to leave she was free to do so.

Angela had been drifting off to sleep as Marie had delivered her purchases and kissed her goodbye, with promises to catch up in September.

The early evening was cool against the antiseptic warmth of the hospital and Marie took a few deep breaths of fresh twilight air.

Her arm felt hot. Marie resisted the urge to rub it. The inflammation would go down if she left it alone, but being in a hospital brought back the memories of her childhood accident and the pain and fear she had felt when her world was collapsing all around her.

Marie strolled over to her car and winding down the windows to create a draught of fresh air sat in the driver's seat. She flipped open her mobile. The only missed message was a text from Ruth.

Gone 2 Maynard's. C U there.

Marie was glad Ruth had saved her the necessity of calling Jed to ask him to return her keys. She texted an acknowledgement to Ruth then made a quick telephone call to her mother.

'Angela's fine,' she assured her. 'She's going back to France the day after tomorrow.'

'I'm so pleased. Now are you sure you're safe to drive back to Maynard's?'

'Absolutely, Mum. I'll call you tomorrow.'

Were other families this complicated? Marie thought as she started the engine and drove carefully out of the car park.

Last night had been a nightmare, one she didn't want to dwell on. Neither did she want to think about what Angela had said about Jed Soames.

Jed was not the sort of man she usually fell for. Admittedly her past choice in men hadn't been brilliant, but stammering undercover agents were hardly her scene either. She switched on the radio. A romantic ballad was playing and its mood matched the balmy evening air and softened Marie's antipathy towards him.

She supposed Jed hadn't fibbed to her that much. Now she came to think about it, she wasn't sure he'd told any lies at all. She couldn't remember exactly what he'd said about being a bodyguard, but Marie should have worked out that Angela wouldn't need one. Had Jed been trying to protect Marie's feelings by not admitting he was investigating Angela's insurance claim? Or had it been his professional integrity?

Ruth liked Jed. Angela liked Jed. Billy respected him. Marie shook her heard. It was no good. Whichever way she looked at it, she was in serious danger of falling in love with him. Yet she'd accused him of heaven knows what.

She hadn't believed him from the first day they'd met up. She'd accused him of breaking into Maynard's, then of hitting himself on the forehead and then she had thrust him out into the night, forcing him to drive all the way to his sister's when he was far from fit. The list of things that had gone wrong between them was endless.

With a sigh, Marie turned into the winding road leading to Rush. It was a lovely feeling coming home, but she must remember Maynard's wasn't her home. As soon as Angela was fit and well again, Marie would have to say goodbye to Ruth and her new friends and then think about her own future.

The call centre beckoned. A small groan escaped Marie's lips as she drove past Ruth's garage, with its bright barrels of bedding plants on the forecourt. The prospect of cold-calling customers as they were about to sit down to their evening meal was grim and would be such a contrast to life here — arguing with Ruth over her lax accounting, sparring with Jed, dealing with aunts who drove their cars into ditches — she had loved every minute of it.

★ ★ ★

The lights were on at Maynard's and beckoned to her through the trees. It was another welcoming sight and gave Marie a warm feeling in the pit of her stomach. She hoped Ruth had the kettle on. After a cup of tea she intended having a warm bath then hours of uninterrupted sleep. She was hardly out of the car before the front door was yanked open, the lights inside cutting a swathe of light across the flagstones.

'You're back,' Ruth rushed down the drive arms outstretched. 'We've been so worried about you.'

'Angela's fine,' Marie began before Ruth enveloped her in a bear hug and almost squeezed the life out of her. 'I can't breathe,' she protested into Ruth's jumper.

'Sorry.' Ruth released her. 'Let me look at you. There are dark circles under your eyes,' she said sternly.

'You'd have them too if you'd spent half the night in a car.'

'What?'

'Let's have some tea and I'll tell you all about it,' Marie said.

'No.' Ruth shook her head, 'we can't.'

'Now what?' Marie felt a shiver of fear inch up her backbone.

'I don't know how to tell you this,' Ruth screwed up her face.

Marie's head began to swim. She was not in the mood for more shocks.

'Can we go inside first?' she asked.

'Come on. You may as well know the worst.' Ruth linked an arm through Marie's and tugged her up the drive.

Pierre was sitting on the sofa in the living room. Jed was standing by the window, a grim look on his face. His green eyes betrayed no emotion as Ruth and Marie came into the room. Marie quelled the small terror of pleasure she felt at seeing him again. From his expression it was obvious her feelings were not reciprocated.

'What's going on?' she asked in a faint voice.

'Marie.' Pierre was his usual charming self. He kissed her on both cheeks.

'How is Angela? Ruth tells me she has been in an accident? She always was a terrible driver. I tell her so many times to watch the road, but does she listen?'

'She's fine,' Marie replied.

'Never mind all that,' Ruth interrupted. 'Tell Marie how you stole her keys from the rack in my garage and then used them to let yourself into Maynard's. Did you know, Marie he watched you key in the security alarm number the other day and memorised it? Talk about sneaky.'

'One thing at a time,' with a voice like ice Jed butted in.

Marie flicked her eyes in his direction. She was so weary she could barely stand up.

'Have you still got the miniatures?' she asked in an expressionless voice.

'Yes. We agreed I would have them valued by a contact of mine.'

'And did you?'

'Yes. They're genuine and . . . '

'Then give them to Pierre, please.'

A stubborn expression stole into

Jed's eyes. 'There are things we have to talk about first,' he insisted.

'I don't think so.' Marie was equally as insistent. 'I have written authority from Angela to pass them over to Pierre.' She searched in her handbag. 'Here.' She thrust the scrap of paper at Jed.

'Will it do? It's not very official but I assure you it's genuine. You can stick it under your microscope or whatever you use, to check Angela's signature.'

Jed took the note from Marie's shaking fingers and glanced at the pencilled note.

'We would need to get it verified,' he said after a slight pause, 'but, yes, that should be fine.'

'Then will you please do as I ask and give the miniatures to Pierre?' Marie repeated her request.

'As you wish.' Jed opened his briefcase and took out the velvet pouch. Without a word he handed it over to Pierre.

With a smile of satisfaction Pierre undid the pouch and inspected the contents.

'They are Dubois miniatures?' Marie asked him.

'Yes. Would you like to receipt Angela's authority?'

He scribbled his name and date on the piece of paper and gave it back to Jed with exaggerated courtesy.

'Thank you, Pierre. Now Jed, I'd like you to leave.'

'But . . . ' he began.

'You too, Ruth.'

'We must talk.' There was a stubborn set to Jed's mouth as if it hurt him to speak.

'Not tonight,' Ruth broke in firmly, taking charge of the situation. 'Can't you see Marie's dead on her feet? Come on, Jed.' She grabbed his arm. 'I'll treat you to some supper. You can pick up your briefcase. Beans on toast do you? I daresay Billy will still be around somewhere. I left him looking after the dogs. He can join us.'

Marie gave her a tired smile. 'Thanks, Ruth. Catch up in the morning?'

'It's a date but not too early. You get a good night's sleep. You hear?' She kissed her on the cheek.

'What about Pierre?' Jed demanded, standing his ground. 'I'm not leaving you alone with him.'

'I assure you, Jed,' Pierre drawled, 'I can be trusted not to attack Marie.' He closed the velvet pouch then placed the miniatures in his own briefcase all the while smiling at Jed. 'Despite your suspicions, I do not attack people in woods.'

'Look,' Ruth attempted to defuse the situation, 'you've got the miniatures and that's all you came for, isn't it?' she asked Pierre.

Pierre gave a quick nod.

'Then come on, Jed. Marie can look after herself and we've outstayed our welcome.'

With no more than a brief glance in her direction, Jed allowed Ruth to hustle him out of the room. Marie waited until she heard Jed's car start up and watched the headlights fade as he drove off before she turned to Pierre.

'So, you do not ask me to leave too? Why is that? Our dinner date still holds if you are interested? Although you do look a little tired.'

'I've a few things to say to you.'

Pierre's smile slipped. 'You're looking very fierce, Marie. What have I done to upset you?'

'We'll overlook the housebreaking at Maynard's.'

'It was all a misunderstanding, Marie, surely you understand? And it wasn't a break in. I had a set of keys — both times. I thought the first set would work, but they didn't.'

'So you decided to hit Jed over the head and steal his?'

'Actually I didn't,' Pierre corrected her with a mocking smile. 'It was that nosey woman and her dog, the one from the bakery, I think? Ruth was telling me about it. They startled Jed, he fell and the dog made off with the case.' He shrugged. 'There you have it. I'm not a housebreaker, Marie believe me.

If I were I would perhaps have made a better job of it. Am I forgiven?'

His brown eyes would have melted a softer heart than Marie's, but she was not in the mood for seduction.

'Not yet. We need to talk about Angela.'

'What has she been saying?' Pierre's eyes narrowed.

'She's been telling me a few things about you and about her operation.'

'I do not understand.' Pierre looked puzzled. 'What has her operation to do with me?'

'Let me enlighten you. If one word about Angela's operation appears in any of the gossip columns you'll have me to deal with.'

'Marie,' Pierre protested, 'let me assure you I am as concerned about Angela's health as you are.'

'Good,' Marie nodded. 'Then I hope that I won't have to put my threat to the test. Do I make myself clear?'

'Of course.' Pierre looked as if the matter were of complete indifference to him.

'I also understand that there have been rumours about how the fire at the chateau was started?'

'That sort of incident always causes rumours.'

'Then perhaps you'd make sure your circle of friends know the true cause of the fire was faulty wiring?'

'We are not certain it was, are we?'

'Otherwise,' Marie ignored his question, 'I might resort to a little blackmail myself.'

Her head was throbbing and she thought longingly of the aromatherapy candles upstairs. Never had the prospect of relaxing in a sunken bath been so inviting.

Threatening people with blackmail was not her scene and although she would never see her threat through, keeping up the pretence was exhausting, but she was blowed if someone like Pierre was going to intimidate Angela.

'And what nature would this blackmail take?' Pierre asked, with a reluctant gleam of respect.

'Copies of paintings being passed off as originals? Something along those lines should fit the bill nicely.'

'That's outrageous, and you know it,' Pierre protested. 'I've never done anything of the sort.'

'Nevertheless,' Marie said with a slow smile, 'mud sticks.'

'You know,' Pierre admitted reluctantly, 'there's more to you than meets the eye.'

'I'm sure we understand each other?' Marie raised an eyebrow. 'So do I have your word? No gossip about Angela?'

Pierre hesitated then nodded and held out his hand. 'You have my word.'

They shook on it.

'Now we are friends again. You are free this evening? Would you like me to stay and keep you company?' Pierre asked. 'I could cook us an intimate dinner a deux?'

'Another time, Pierre.' Marie yawned, making her eyes water. 'Tonight I'm going to follow Ruth's example and make myself beans on toast.'

'I can't tempt you to my very good chicken in white wine sauce?'

Marie shook her head. 'Let yourself out will you?'

Pierre sighed, looking disappointed. 'In that case I will wish you goodnight and sweet dreams, my pretty cousin.'

He embraced her, then picking up his briefcase containing the miniatures sauntered out of the room.

Marie waited until she heard the throb of his powerful exhausts departing down the drive before locking the door, setting the alarm then heading for the stairs and the sunken bath.

Ruth Tries To Bring
Marie And Jed Together

'Sorry,' Ruth apologised, 'Marie hasn't turned up for work yet. I expect she's catching up on her sleep. She'll probably be in later.' She smiled up at Jed. 'Do you need a receipt?'

Jed handed over his cheque and his mother's bill. 'It can wait,' he replied.

Ruth frowned up at him. 'You're looking tired too. Is that bump on the head still giving you trouble?'

'I didn't get much sleep last night,' Jed acknowledged, 'and we had a couple of disrupted days before that.'

'You can say that again,' Ruth agreed. 'Anyway I'm glad everything turned out right in the end with Angela and Pierre and the miniatures,' she said.

'Yes,' Jed's face was giving nothing

away as he said, 'that's my job done here then.'

'What exactly were you doing?' Ruth asked, 'I mean I know it's absolutely none of my business, but all that secret service nonsense wasn't true, was it?'

'I don't know how that story got about.' Jed looked mildly irritated.

'It all started when you leapt out from behind a bush and frightened the wits out of Marie, I seem to recall,' Ruth teased him, 'or have I got my wires crossed?'

Jed ignored the jibe.

'I was asked to help go through some aspects of Angela's claim. In places it was very — er, creative.'

'I've never met Angela, but I feel sorry for her,' Ruth sympathised. 'Imagine if there was a fire here.' She looked round the office at the piles of paperwork, now neatly stacked and collated and shuddered. 'I wouldn't have a clue what was missing.'

'Well, it's up to the French authorities to sort out the rest of the claim now,' Jed said. 'My brief was to track down the miniatures. There'll be a lot of paperwork to catch up on, but I don't see a problem. Angela's note giving authority for Pierre to have them should be sufficient for insurance purposes so that part of the claim can be written off.'

'Are all your jobs as exciting as this one?' Ruth raised an eyebrow. 'I mean attempted break ins, fires, missing miniatures.' Her eyes danced with amusement, 'not to mention beautiful nieces appearing on the scene and stealing your heart. Don't look at me like that, Jed Soames. I've known you far too long to be scared by a glare from my best friend's kid brother.'

'I am not glaring,' Jed began, but Ruth was on a roll and not listening.

'Biddy hasn't had so much to gossip about in years.'

'Yes, well,' Jed interrupted her, 'I only dropped by to give you my cheque, so if there's nothing else?' His voice was clipped and did not invite further confidence.

'Aren't you going to stay and have a quick word with Marie?' Ruth asked.

'She's not here.'

'I'm sure she'll be in shortly.'

'Then can you ask her to send me my mother's receipt through the post as usual?'

'I wasn't talking about your mother's bill,' Ruth snapped.

'Weren't you?'

'I was talking about you and Marie.'

'What about us?'

'For heaven's sake, Jed. Do I have to spell it out?'

A small muscle quivered under Jed's eye. 'Y . . . yes, you do.'

'How long have I known you?' Ruth demanded. 'No, don't answer. It wasn't a rhetorical question. What I'm trying to say is, why can't the pair of you get together like . . . ' Ruth groped around for a suitable simile.

'You and Billy?' Jed queried with a reluctant smile.

'Well, yes.'

Ruth glanced down at her solitaire ring with a smile. 'I haven't told Marie my news yet. There wasn't a chance last night. I wouldn't normally wear my ring in the workshop, but I wanted to show it to her. I'll take it off later. Don't want to damage it.'

Jed smiled at Ruth with affection as she waggled her ring finger at him.

'Not all of us are as blessed as you and Billy,' he said.

'That's nonsense,' Ruth replied gruffly.

'Maybe, but it's true.'

'Are you trying to tell me there's nothing between you and Marie?'

'N . . . no,' he replied.

'I'm not sure what you're denying, but let me tell you, Jed Soames, if you don't do something soon you'll let Marie slip through your fingers.'

'I rather think Pierre might have got in there first.'

'Pierre?' Ruth's voice was now full of scorn. 'You can't think he and Marie are an item?'

'I seem to recall you and I were

hustled out of Maynard's very quickly last night and Marie couldn't wait to return his miniatures to him.'

'Aren't they his and didn't she have Angela's authority to pass them over?' Ruth demanded.

'Yes,' Jed admitted reluctantly.

'Well, then, what is all the fuss about?'

'I'm not the one making the fuss,' Jed said. 'You were the one who first brought up the subject.'

'Only because I can't bear to see the two of you tiptoeing around each other. You do love Marie, don't you?' Ruth demanded bluntly.

A crimson wash of colour rose up Jed's face. 'That's none of your business.'

'I'll take that as a yes, then. Now, what are you going to do about it?'

'Will you please stop interfering in my affairs, Ruth?'

'No, I won't. Somebody has to knock some sense into the pair of you.'

A sound outside disturbed the tense

silence that had fallen between the pair of them.

'Who's there?' Ruth called out from the office.

'Only me. What are you doing in here?' Marie poked her head around the door. Her eyes looked brighter than last night and the worry lines had disappeared from her face. 'Sorry I'm late. I overslept.' Her eyes fell on Jed. She stiffened. 'Am I interrupting something?'

'While you've been lying around in bed I've been doing your job,' Ruth replied. 'Now you are here you can receipt Jed's bill for him.'

Marie shrugged off her coat. 'Of course.'

The summer dress she was wearing clung to her slender frame, emphasising her feminine curves. Ruth hid a smile as she saw the effect her innocent gesture of hanging up her coat had on Jed. His eyes never left her back.

'Here,' Ruth held up the rubber stamp as Marie turned round. 'By the way,' she added, 'what do you think of this?' The sunlight caught the facets of her diamond ring.

'She's been dying to show it off to you all morning,' Jed said with an indulgent smile. 'She nearly had my eye out with it the other day.'

Marie looked from Ruth to Jed then back to Ruth again as the full implication of his words sunk in.

'You're engaged?' Marie's raised voice had Honey racing into the office barking frantically at all the disruption.

'Now look what you've done,' Ruth grumbled with a beaming smile as a pile of invoices was swept to the floor by the swing of Honey's excited tale.

Marie ignored the mess and leaning across the desk, hugged Ruth. 'I couldn't be more pleased. Why didn't you tell me last night? It is Billy, isn't it?'

'There were other more pressing issues last night, and of course it's Billy. Will you be quiet?' she bellowed at a thoroughly over excited Honey who was now threatening to topple the rest of the invoices. 'Jed, grab hold of her collar, will you?'

After a brief struggle Jed managed to gain control of Honey who licked his hand ecstatically and panted up at him.

'Why don't I leave you two to catch up?' he said to Ruth. 'Come on, Honey. Outside.'

'No. Wait.' Ruth leapt out of the seat she had been occupying behind Marie's desk. 'I'll take her. I'm sure you two have things you'd like to talk about. I'll go and make some tea.'

Before either Marie or Jed could stop her, Ruth had dragged a reluctant Honey out of the office. Her paws scraped the hard surface of the floor as she tried, without success, to dig herself in. Ruth closed the door firmly behind her.

'Good news, isn't it?' Marie smiled at Jed. 'I'm so pleased for Ruth. They'll be so happy together, Ruth bossing Billy and Billy pretending to grumble but secretly loving it.'

'Yes,' Jed agreed. His smile lingered in his eyes as he looked at Marie, before clearing his throat and transferring his attention back to the desk. 'I brought my mother's bill in for you to deal with.'

'The receipt. Yes, of course.' The smile left Marie's face. 'What happened to the stamp?'

'I don't know. Ruth had it.'

'It's here, on the floor.' Marie pointed to where it had rolled under a chair. 'She must have dropped it.'

Their fingers grazed as they both bent down to pick it up. Marie flinched at the feel of Jed's fingers against hers.

'Sorry,' he apologised, 'I didn't realise the touch of my flesh was so unwelcome.'

Marie staggered to her feet, her cheeks flaming. 'It's not that.'

'Her head was swimming. After a hot bath and a good night's sleep, she'd got her senses back into some sort of order and it was on the drive down to Ruth's she realised that Jed could be walking out of her life forever. She wasn't sure how things stood between them but she did know this might be her last chance to do anything about it.'

'I, er . . . ' she began, then watched Jed stamp his mother's invoice.

'If you'll initial and date it, that will be fine.'

'About Pierre,' Marie began, ignoring the piece of paper Jed had thrust under her nose.

He shook his head dismissively.

'What you get up to with Pierre is none of my business.'

'I only wanted to explain how things stand between us.'

'Between you and Pierre or between you and me?'

'You're not making this easy for me, Jed,' Marie began. 'Last night I was tired and . . . '

'Not too tired to spend time with Pierre.'

'That's a disgraceful thing to say,' Marie retaliated. 'I had personal matters to discuss with Pierre, which were nothing to do with you.'

'My thoughts exactly,' Jed agreed. 'What you get up to in your private life is nothing to do with me. Now I've a busy morning ahead of me . . . '

'Pierre is family. Angela was worried about something and I needed to talk it through with Pierre. That's the only reason I asked you and Ruth to leave. Ruth's not being huffy about it, so why should you?'

'Tea,' Ruth's cheerful voice broke into the scene. 'For goodness sake what's the matter with you this morning?' she demanded as Honey wove between her legs. 'You'll have me over. Could you take the tray please, Jed?' She held it out towards him, 'before I come a cropper?'

He placed it carefully on the desk.

'I won't stay for tea, thanks, Ruth.' He edged past Honey. 'I've been out of the office for days and I've got a huge backlog of paperwork to catch up on.'

Ruth looked from him to Marie and took in the situation at a glance. 'Before you go,' she began, detaining Jed in the doorway. 'Billy and I are holding an engagement party on Friday. We'd like you to come.'

'I'm er,' Jed hesitated then said, 'thank you, I'd like that.'

'Good, because I'm not taking any excuses. You're invited too of course, Marie,' Ruth looked across to where Marie was still standing by the desk. 'In fact,' she beamed as if struck by a brilliant idea, 'why don't I drive us all over?'

'I wouldn't hear of it,' Marie protested. 'It's your party, you can't be the driver.'

'I never drink anything stronger than orange juice. It always goes to my head. Now, we're holding the party at that hotel you know the one where Pierre was doing his deal with the miniatures? Billy was impressed by their party package and dropped in to have a chat with them and booked it all up.'

'I'll make my own way over,' Jed replied, 'but thanks for the offer, Ruth.'

'Any time from nine o'clock onwards then. Don't be late, otherwise the food will be gone.'

Marie picked up a mug of tea and cast a look at Jed. 'Have you invited Pierre?' she asked Ruth.

'I hadn't actually,' Ruth admitted, 'but if he's staying at the hotel, I suppose it would be rude not to. He'll be very welcome. I think he and Billy have sorted out their differences about the painting and it's about time we all moved on.'

'My thoughts entirely,' Marie nodded. 'I'll phone him and tell him about the party then, shall I? I'm looking forward to seeing him again. Are you having music, Ruth? I should imagine Pierre's a lovely dancer.'

There was a faint movement from Jed in the doorway. 'Sorry?' Marie asked with a teasing look in her eye. 'Did you say something?'

Jed's face was expressionless as he shook his head.

'Don't worry about giving me a lift

home,' Marie said turning her attention back to Ruth. 'You'll want to stay on with Billy. I'm sure I can fix something up with Pierre.'

She began dialling the hotel number. When she looked up from the telephone Jed had gone.

'Now see what you've done.' Ruth glared at her.

'What?' Twin spots of colour stained Marie's cheeks.

'Honestly, you're worse than a pair of children. Well, I've done my best. The rest is up to you,' Ruth said then stomped out of the office.

I'd Say You Were Jealous

Fairy lights dangled from the trees surrounding the terrace and candle flames flickered from inside pastel coloured bell jars placed on all the tables.

'I didn't realise you knew so many people, Ruth.' Marie looked round the throngs of partygoers who had spilled out from the ballroom on to the lawn.

Strains of music drifted through the French windows. Marie caught a glimpse of laughing couples dancing energetically to an old sixties hit.

'A lot of them are Billy's contacts,' Ruth said, waving to yet another arrival. 'I'd better go and do my hostess duties. I don't like to leave you on your own. Are you sure you'll be all right?' She squeezed Marie's elbow.

'Of course I will. After all we've been through recently I'm sure I can look after myself at an engagement party. They look a pretty friendly lot. Don't worry about me. Now,' Marie gave Ruth a friendly push, 'enjoy.'

She watched Ruth weave her way across the lawn towards Billy, a tiny lump forming at the back of her throat. They looked so happy together as they welcomed their guests, and laughed and joked with their friends. Marie couldn't help feeling a pang of envy.

If only she could talk to Jed, maybe they could re-establish their relationship, but she hadn't seen him since that day in Ruth's office and she couldn't think of a good enough reason to contact him.

'Marie,' Pierre greeted her as he appeared at her side clutching two flutes of chilled champagne. 'You do not have a drink. Allow me to offer you one of these. I saw you standing on your own and that I cannot allow.'

'Thank you.'

'Blue suits you.' He smiled into her eyes.

'You too.' The fresh cotton fabric of his shirt was a strong contrast to the depth of his tan.

Marie had chosen her dress with care but there was no sign of Jed and she was beginning to grow annoyed with herself for having taken so much trouble. She tossed back her hair. So what if he wasn't here? She could have a good time without him.

'So Ruth and her Billy are engaged,' Pierre said. 'It was kind of Ruth to invite me to their party. Last year Billy and I were not so — friendly over that business with the painting. It was a genuine mistake, you know.'

'Billy won't hold a grudge,' Marie assured him, 'and I'm sure Ruth will keep an eye on things from now on.'

'They go together well, don't they?'

'They do and I'm convinced they'll be very happy.'

'You are not with Jed tonight?' Pierre asked, scanning the crowd. 'I do not see him here.'

'I came with Ruth,' Marie said.

Pierre looked thoughtful. 'That is a pity.'

'Why?'

'I thought maybe the two of you?' He raised a querying eyebrow.

'I don't want to talk about Jed.'

'As you wish. Have you heard from Angela?' Pierre asked.

'I had a text. She is back in France and suffered no ill effect from her accident, but she's going to take things easy for a week or two.'

'I too will be going back to France tomorrow.'

'So soon?'

'My business here is finished and I have been away long enough.' Pierre paused. 'I have to tell you, I sold the miniatures.'

'Why?'

'I had a good offer for them and I needed the money,' Pierre said simply.

'But aren't they a family heirloom?'

'To be honest they were not worth very much and my father would not have minded. In many ways we understood each other. That was why we argued so often. It was good we had Angela to act as a, how do you say, buffer?'

'Yes, that's the word.'

'I needed the money because my girlfriend is threatening to leave me.' He waved to someone over Marie's shoulder. 'She wants to get married so we will have to move into a bigger flat.'

'Married?' Marie's eyes were wide with surprise.

'Perhaps next spring? I think it's a good time to settle down, don't you?'

'Isn't this rather sudden?'

'There is no need to wait now I have sold the miniatures,' Pierre looked round. 'We could have an engagement party too. What do you think?'

'Er, yes. It's a good idea.'

'To us?' Pierre held up his glass and Marie chinked hers against his.

'We haven't known each other long I agree, but . . . Jed. Hello.' He broke into a smile of welcome, 'I didn't see you standing there.'

Marie spun round to face him. Jed too was wearing smart casual. His shirt was pristine white and open at the neck. If it hadn't been for the patch of hair around his bruise, which was growing back spiky he would almost have matched Pierre for laid back cool.

Marie would have liked to flatten his hair back into place. She didn't think she had ever seen him look so heart wrenchingly unattainable.

'Darling,' Pierre waved to someone in the crowd of partygoers. 'Can I leave Marie in your tender care, Jed?' he asked with his charming smile. 'I should network.'

Pierre kissed Marie on the cheek. There was an unspoken message in his eyes that left Marie with the suspicion that Pierre had somehow manipulated this encounter with Jed.

'So, congratulations are in order?' Jed's voice was flat.

'Yes.' Marie looked across the lawn. 'Have you seen Ruth and Billy? They were around a minute ago.'

'I'm not talking about Ruth and Billy.'

Marie raised her eyebrows. 'You're not?'

'I suppose I should also congratulate Pierre.'

'Yes — what a surprise that was.'

'It's also very convenient.'

Marie frowned. 'What is?'

'It keeps things in the family. Will you move to France?'

'Jed, what exactly are you talking about?'

'It's quite simple. Now your work at Maynard's is more or less finished, will you move to France?'

'Why?'

'To be with Pierre.'

'Why should I want to be with Pierre?'

'Correct me if I'm wrong, but hasn't he just proposed to you?'

'Proposed, to me?' A bubble of laughter built up inside Marie.

At that moment she caught sight of Pierre in the crowd of partygoers. He turned and winked at her. Marie couldn't resist a little wave in his direction. Her suspicions were correct. Pierre must have spotted Jed over her shoulder and set the whole thing up.

'What's so funny?' Jed demanded.

'You are. If I didn't know you better, I'd say you were jealous.'

'Over Pierre?' Jed could hardly keep the scorn out of his voice.

'There's no need to be, you know.' Marie took pity on him and held up a hand before Jed could interrupt. 'He didn't ask me to marry him.'

'D . . . didn't ask you?' Jed repeated. 'But I distinctly heard him say . . . '

'I don't know what you thought you heard him say, Jed,' she touched his arm lightly. The muscles felt firm under her fingers, 'but you were wrong. He was telling me he sold the miniatures to release some funds, so that he could get married to his girlfriend. If you don't believe me, ask him yourself.'

'You're not getting married to Pierre?'

'No. Not now. Not ever.' Marie

smiled up into Jed's confused eyes, emboldened she suggested, 'so that leaves you and me, doesn't it?'

'Does it?' Jed's confusion was replaced with a wary look.

Marie tweaked the collar of his shirt. 'As you seem reluctant to commit, I'll put it in words you'll understand, shall I?' She watched in satisfaction as a small muscle began to quiver under Jed's left eye. 'Don't things go in threes?' she asked.

'W . . . what sort of things?'

'Well, there's Ruth and Billy, and Pierre and his girlfriend, and now there's you and me.'

'Darling.' Marie jumped as a female voice sliced through the evening air. A very beautiful blonde woman smiled into Jed's eyes and curled an arm possessively around his shoulders, 'Sorry I made us late arriving, but now I've freshened up I simply must go and speak to Ruth and Billy. Get me a drink. There's a good boy. Hello, who's this? No, introductions to your friend will have to wait.'

The green eyes were full of amusement, as they looked up and down Marie. 'I've just spotted one of the gang in the crowd, must go and have a word. Why don't you join me in a minute?'

Marie flinched as though she'd been stung and watched the female ruffle Jed's hair, kiss his left ear then stroll away across the lawn.

Jed's mouth quirked into a half smile as he waited for Marie to speak.

Marie's eyes narrowed. 'No wonder you haven't been in touch,' she began. 'How many other females have you got in tow?'

'Now who's jealous?' Jed teased, his eyes dancing with laughter.

'I'm not jealous of . . . '

'Careful what you say,' Jed advised her, 'I'm really quite fond of Suzie and it doesn't do to get undignified.'

'And how long have you known Suzie?'

'Quite a while. We live together on and off.'

'Jed.' There was a blurred flash of aquamarine silk as Ruth flung her arms round his neck and kissed him on the cheek. 'You made it. I was beginning to think you weren't going to come. Did I just see Suzie?'

'You did.' Jed was having difficulty trying to stand upright from the enthusiasm of Ruth's greeting.

'Great. I haven't seen the old trout in ages. Where'd she go?'

'I think she was looking for you.'

'Have you introduced her to Marie?'

'Not yet.'

'You'll absolutely adore Jed's sister,' Ruth grinned at Marie. 'She's a bit bossy, but underneath all that she's got a heart of gold. See you.'

Jed's slow smile curved into laughter. 'You should see the expression on your face,' he teased her. 'You've gone all twitchy and pink like a rabbit.'

'I suppose you think that's funny,' Marie hissed at him, feeling hot and foolish.

'No funnier than you pretending to be engaged to Pierre.'

'I was not pretending anything. You

overheard us talking and formed your own conclusions.'

'The same way you did with me and Suzie?'

Marie opened her mouth to protest then saw the way Jed was looking at her and broke into a smile.

'Shall we call it quits?' she asked.

'Good idea,' Jed agreed, 'if you promise me you're really not engaged to Pierre?'

'Promise,' Marie agreed solemnly, 'and to put the record straight, the only reason I made him stay on at Maynard's the other night was because I thought he'd upset Angela and I wanted him to know that if he did it again, he'd have me and my mother to reckon with as well.'

'Scary stuff,' Jed acknowledged.

'Pierre also apologised for frightening me over that break in business. He knew the miniatures were in Angela's things and he wanted them back. Anyway we cleared the air and we're friends now.'

'Good,' Jed nodded.

'By the way, he says on the night of the ball he was nowhere near Maynard's so it couldn't have been him who attacked you.'

Jed shuffled his feet. 'Actually it was Biddy's dog.'

'So the story about the briefcase is true?' Marie began to laugh.

'Turns out she leapt up at me, I dropped my briefcase and banged my head on . . . are you laughing at me again?'

'Just as well you're not a private bodyguard, if you can't hold your own against a dog.'

'Why don't we talk about something else?'

'Looks like I was right all along about you banging your head, doesn't it?' Marie held up her hands. 'All right. I won't tease you any more. Sorry.'

'So there really is nothing between you and Pierre?'

'No.' Marie paused. 'That night at Maynard's?' she began. 'Not the night of the ball, but the one when Angela arrived.'

'Do you mean,' Marie didn't think she'd ever heard Jed's voice so husky, 'the one when I kissed you?'

Marie was glad they were in the garden of the hotel and Jed couldn't see the flames of colour shoot up her face. She cleared her throat self-consciously.

'Yes, that's the one I mean,' she replied.

'Then I have to tell you, I'd rather like to kiss you again.'

'You would?'

Marie's eyes flashed to Jed's face. Quite without her realising it, he seemed to have moved into her body space. She could almost feel the strength of his muscles against her body, even though they weren't physically touching each other.

If Marie's heel hadn't sunk into the soft grass she would have taken a step backwards. As it was, she couldn't move.

'You can't kiss me here,' she protested.

'Why not?' Jed asked, 'it's a party, isn't it?'

'There are too many people about.'

'We could always go somewhere quieter.'

'We can't leave Ruth's party,' Marie protested.

'To discuss our future.'

'Future?' Marie said in a faint echo.

'Yours and mine and in order to avoid any further misunderstandings, I have to tell you I'm offering you a job.'

'A job?' Marie's raised voice drew several interested glances in her direction.

'I wish you'd stop repeating everything I say. Now,' Jed put a hand to her lips. 'Listen to me for a moment. It's unpaid. The hours are long. I can be very grumpy first thing in the morning. Holidays may be disrupted at a moment's notice,' he paused, 'and you're not allowed to leave under any circumstances. What do you say?'

'What exactly is the nature of this job?' Marie's voice was almost as husky now as Jed's.

'I'm asking you to marry me,' Jed said, 'before Pierre changes his mind and decides he wants to marry you after all.'

'You don't mind inheriting an erratic aunt and a mother who will insist on interfering in our lives?'

'We've got several erratic aunts in our family too and my mother's pretty good on the interfering scene as well, ask Suzie. Now,' he continued, 'If you can't think up any further objections, what's your answer and I have to tell you I'll keep asking you until you come up with the answer I like.'

Marie looked into his battered face and taking a finger to his forehead she stroked his bruise.

'I accept,' she said softly.

Out of the corner of her eye she caught sight of Ruth and Suzie dancing a jig of delight by the water feature.

'What's going on, girls?' Billy demanded. 'Can anyone join in?'

'My baby brother's just asked Marie to marry him,' Suzie announced to everyone, 'and she's accepted.'

A ragged cheer broke out.

Jed raised his eyes in annoyance at the sound of his sister's excited voice.

'Hadn't you better introduce me properly to Suzie?' Marie smiled.

'She can wait,' Jed said, 'right now I've got better things to do. Now where was I?'

Leaning forward he drew Marie into his arms and kissed her.

THE END